LUMENS

A GHOST STORY

MARY JANE CAPPS

For the ghosts and the girls who know them

CHAPTER ONE

My sister is dead, and I'm pretty sure it's my fault.

I think my parents would agree.

I've said my goodbyes to the few friends who matter—Melinda and Drew, basically.

I take a second to breathe in the wet pavement and tobacco, the smells of hot dogs and car exhaust floating into the open window before I shut and lock it. Anything to clear out the heady perfume that lingers in Veronica's room. It just won't leave.

Like her memory.

It's stronger than any bond we ever had in life.

Even though she'd officially moved out a year ago to share a tiny studio apartment with two other dancers, she'd been as good as gone years before.

You don't get to be the youngest Rockette by vegging on

the couch with your kid sister, reading mystery novels. You don't get to be a star by staying in, staying ordinary.

I can't catch the salt on my tongue in Manhattan the way I can a gritty snowflake. You have to get out to shore to taste the brine.

My dad forces a smile on his tight lips as he zips my suitcase closed. My mom won't look me in the eyes as she hands me a muffin for the road.

I can barely remember the last time we visited Sayers Beach.

The waves were so big they threatened to wash me out to sea.

My dad had left his laptop back at my aunt and uncle's place, at my mother's insistence. He had spent the afternoon looking at the ocean with me. My mother transformed me into a mermaid in the sand. I helped her choose the perfect shells for her art collage. She even gave me credit on the little plaque pasted next to it when it hung weeks later on the gallery wall.

Ver took the sun when she could get it.

We called Veronica that, Ver like *very*.

She found the only boy her age on the beach—or should I say he found her? She glittered like that, unmissable.

We ate lobster and wore silly bibs. I teased Veronica when she couldn't crack the shell right, and lobster juice squirted her in the face. I laughed and I wasn't afraid of annoying her. She gave me a smile bright as the rays on the shore.

I knew it was special, this ease with her, with us. It didn't come often. I didn't expect it, so when I was small, I savored it.

I kept the memory, the feeling close to hold me over when the smile changed and the light turned away from me.

She couldn't help it; it was just how she was. That's what my dad said once, when I was eleven and I asked him about the way things were with her and me, the way we felt all scrambled up and far away. When I still asked questions.

"It's just her way, Libby, hang on." His thumb had drifted across his phone screen so fast I felt like he was only partly with me. "Since she could crawl, she's been going somewhere. Even *our* family isn't exciting enough for Ver." He laughed a stilted laugh, his eyes flickering back to the screen and resting there.

"John." My mother was in the corner, attempting to crochet something, her head resting against the wall.

"Oh, sorry." My dad yanked his eyes away from his phone, planting them once more upon me. "Work. You understand."

He reached out and pulled me into his lap. I was too big for it, I thought at the time, but I lay my head against his narrow shoulder, the light from the phone blooming over our faces, the candle before my mother casting a shadow across her quietly cursing lips as she tossed her needlework aside and grabbed her scissors and paper for comfort.

It was comfortable when it was just the three of us. I

remember I made a silent wish that it could always be that way.

I dig through the tote bag beside me in the back of our Subaru. *Death in the Library*, *Death in the Graveyard*, *Death in the Garden*—a good murder mystery is usually like a cozy blanket, but in the blur of these last couple months, I can't take all the death. I reach for one of my mom's books instead —the kinds of things you see in the supermarket stand, where someone has rippling abs and someone else's dress is conveniently torn across billowing cleavage, and everyone knows the young countess just wants to be with the young stable hand.

Yawn.

Our path through Upstate New York is lined with pines like fortress walls.

Stretches like this one open up to a view of the sea as we move endlessly through Connecticut. I'm boarding a small airplane out of Hartford. I don't know why I'm not flying out of Newark or JFK. Maybe because it's a four-hour flight, and my parents suddenly feel weird about their fifteen-year-old being unsupervised for that long. They didn't used to, but things change. Or they still love a good road trip.

Except my dad isn't blasting Zeppelin. My mom isn't suggesting silly games. They pass the time in silence. We all do. Like I said, I'm done asking questions.

I wonder if my appetite for ghost stories is weakened because now I can't shake this haunted feeling. It inches up my back and presses on the once-quiet places in my brain.

It's not fun or spine-tingling or even eerie.

It's heavy and relentless.

Not at all like the bright, luminous spirit of my sister.

It's not her at all.

More like the ghost of regret, sticking with me now in the backseat, in the shower, in my blankets when I lie down to sleep.

Definitely when I receive the text reminder.

Ding!

It pulls me out of my thoughts, and then takes me right back to them.

I lift my phone to read what I know is already there.

2 p.m.: Check on Ver.

"Who's texting you, babe?" My mother attempts to sound normal from the front seat, like she and my dad aren't dropping me off at a remote beach so they can forget about me and everything my presence makes them remember.

"Just Melinda. Saying bye again."

I didn't used to lie. I used to tell my parents everything. About me, and about Veronica. Well, everything I could gather on her.

"It'll be good, babe." My mom turns and reaches her hand back, like she's done since I was in a car seat. I hesitate, then take it, giving her bony fingers a gentle squeeze.

It's more about reassuring her.

"You need this," my dad says.

No, you need this. I stare through the window, wanting to jump out and run across the traffic, skip from car to car, jump into the ocean just outside, swim to anywhere.

That desire doesn't leave me on the plane. It doesn't leave me at the airport when Uncle Frank meets me.

He looks almost exactly like the Gorton's fisherman in the frozen-food aisle, minus the yellow raincoat. He's wearing a faded T-shirt and khaki shorts. He's my dad's uncle, really, my great-uncle.

"Libby." He reaches out to take my massive suitcase and duffel bag in one huge callused fist, and uses the other hand to give my shoulders a double pat. "I'm glad to see you."

I smile weakly. No one says anything more as we load up his truck and drive fifty miles to Sayers Beach.

The inn is like a weathered postcard image.

Salt-beaten white boards frame a house on the edge of the peninsula, and a stretch of land juts off to the east, opening up to the lighthouse. It's a ghostly white tower with a midnight blue top.

I stop when I see it and do what I used to, counting the seconds . . . one . . . three . . . five . . . and then the spotlight flashes over me, just for a second, and slips away again, turning in its constant rotation.

The home is all theirs—Uncle Frank's and Aunt Sharon's—but the lighthouse belongs to the Sayers Beach Historical Society. My uncle and aunt just take care of it.

Mainly Aunt Sharon. She's on the board of the society, I think, and she manages the inn. She spills out of the doorway, oblivious to the screen door whacking a girl on her way out, and comes barreling toward me with a cookie the size of my face.

"Libby-Lib!" *Ugh. She's still saying that?*

Uncle Frank has a death grip on my luggage as he rounds up the line—me in the middle, Sharon in the lead, and the victim of the slammed door sucking her finger beside the cement stoop.

The front of the place is unassuming. It would seem run-down, but the peeling paint is masked by huge lavender bushes and climbing roses arching up the wrought-iron railing. We step inside, and it smells like a confusion of scented candles—there's a different one in each room.

The girl with the sore finger, who seems to be housekeeping, is wisely opening the thin-paned windows to let the salt air in. Sharon ushers me into the kitchen while Frank disappears with my suitcases.

I've only had a bite of the cookie when she pushes coffee cake in front of me, her long arms and neck reminding me of a giraffe with a bleached-blonde bob. *Does she eat all this stuff? How is she so skinny?*

A flash of Veronica accepting every treat she was offered enters my mind. She would always accept the cookie, take one bite, then spit it out in her napkin later.

"Why do you take it when you don't eat sugar?" I remember asking.

"Don't *swallow* sugar," Ver corrected me. She would say things like that and just leave them, as if they were an actual answer.

"Coffee with cream? Like your parents?"

"No . . ." I haven't drunk coffee much. I haven't anything much. I clear my throat. "Black please. That's how I take it."

"Sugar, then?"

"Just black."

"It's decaf since it's so late." She brings it to me, and it turns out that coffee without cream and sugar is like drinking steaming dirt. But there's no turning back now. I gag a little from the bitter punch.

"How is it, Libby?"

"A little weak." I shrug.

"Ah." She squints her eyes for a fraction of a second.

"You've got some new signs." I've counted about five new ones. She's always had the enormous "Live, Laugh, Love" painted on a canvas above the table, ordering guests to enjoy every freaking precious moment, and one that says "Dance Like No One's Watching" with a mermaid and merguy(?) attempting a tango. But now she's got "Today's a Gift. That's Why They Call It the Present" with a smiling starfish and a plaque that says "Life Is Better at the Beach" hanging over one of those sparkly Thomas Kinkade lighthouse paintings that makes my Brooklyn-artist mom want to throw up.

Aunt Sharon dumps a cup of cream and sugar into her own mug.

I cringe as she sits down, waiting for her to say something stupid, like "Poor Veronica. Heaven needed another angel!" But she just gulps her coffee.

Then she reaches out and squeezes my limp hand. "I'm so sorry."

I nod, and we sit like that until Uncle Frank returns and mutters something about showing me the trick to the sticky doorknob on my bedroom door.

The two of them escort me up and wish me goodnight. I don't bother to unpack, don't even bother to put on pajamas. I just wrap myself around a pillow and wait for morning.

"Housekeeping." There's a short knock on my door. I open it to find the girl that I saw get smacked by the screen door.

"I'm sorry?"

We are on the other side of the house from the guests, down a hall divided by a sliding wooden door that likes to hop off its tracks. Over here it's Frank and Sharon's room, Sharon's tiny "craft room," (I think it used to be a closet) and the guest room—my room. All the inn guests stay on the opposite side of the sliding door in the three other rooms.

"Kidding. You clean your own room." She offers a thin half smile. She looks a little bit older than me. "I'm Marnie." She eyes me, raising one hand in a small wave.

I offer a shrug in return. I guess it's my thing now. "Libby."

"I know."

"Oh."

"Ever eat Greek breakfast?"

"No."

"Come with me."

"Okay, let me just get dressed first."

Marnie looks over my slept-in clothes and cocks an eyebrow.

I clear my throat and close the door, gently, in her face.

I rummage through my still-unpacked suitcase and grab clean underwear and a black tank top. *Fine. Perfect.* Not looking to make a statement here.

I spot something out of the corner of my eye.

My necklace. Floating in the window. The jagged half of my sister's broken charm. It was a nine-point star with the word "Polaris" carved into a banner attached to the bottom; now it's four points of a star and the letters "Pola." It is suspended from its chain, hanging from the lock on the windowsill.

It shouldn't be there. It should be on the bedside table beside the antique lamp, right where I set it last night. I had laid it on the bedside table before I shut the light off.

Now it's dangling in the window, the thin chain resting on the metal lock

My heart pounds. I flip to rage. *How dare they?*

How dare who, Libby?

I bound across the room in two strides and reach for my necklace, unable to guess why anyone would, or how anyone *could*, have snuck into my room at night, picked up my dead sister's necklace, and hung it from the windowsill.

I am the lightest sleeper in the world.

My fingers tingle as I grab hold of the half-star charm and lift it.

The lighthouse looms straight ahead, not eighty yards away.

"Oh, are you going out with Libby today?" My aunt's voice in the hall brings me back. I turn to the mirror, clasp the necklace around my throat, and run a brush through my light brown hair.

I close my eyes and take a long breath.

When I open the door again, Marnie's standing, unmoved, hand on her hip. *Did Aunt Sharon send her to be my playmate? Does she still think I'm seven?*

Marnie's eyes are a deep dark brown, and she has an unnerving gaze. I wish she would stop looking at me.

She finally does, pivoting on a foot and bouncing down the stairs. I follow her slowly, silently, my hand on the rail.

Not looking to rush for pals.

Marnie waits at the bottom of the stairs as I glide down as elegantly as I can. I'm like Scarlett at Tara.

"You hurt or something?" Marnie knits her eyebrows together and sets her laser eyes on my ankles.

"No." I stiffen, then pick up the pace. I follow her wordlessly out the door, into the smell of salt and pine and sunshine.

"This is a Greek breakfast?" I ask, eyeing my fat bagel heaped with cream cheese. Something familiar to home.

"Would you prefer yogurt and honey with grapes and nuts?" A boy about my age with pale eyes, dark hair, and a slightly crooked smile speaks the words so softly it's hard to hear him over the chatter of patrons and the hum of phony laughter from the morning talk-show hosts on the TV mounted above the counter.

I lift my warm, toasty bagel to my lips and take a bite. The cream cheese softens between my teeth.

"No." Veronica would. Minus the yogurt. And honey. And nuts. She'd pretty much eat a grape.

"Chop, chop, Nicky!" Marnie snaps her fingers and laughs, and the boy wipes his hands on his apron, picks up a coffee pot out of the Bunn maker, and begins refilling the cup of the old man engrossed in his paper.

"Fine." Marnie hoists herself out of our pleather cushioned booth and glides behind the counter. "I'll take that, thank you!" She reaches for the pot and fills two mugs. She murmurs something, and I look away quickly when the boy looks at me in interest.

The coffee is strong. I'm on the second half of my bagel while Marnie chats with a woman behind her.

I can feel eyes on me. It's more than one pair.

The summer crowd hasn't boomed yet, since it's early June.

They must be wondering who I am.

A voice breaks my discomfort.

"Libby? I know Sharon and Frank—I'm Sarah." The woman looks weathered, old. "We're doing a lobster boil tonight down at the VFW and fire station. Come on by. It's a big hit!"

Sounds thrilling. "Uh, I might have a thing. To do."

"We're all going." Marnie stares at me. "Me, my cousin, Nicky." She points at the aproned boy who's come to clear my plate. Seeing him up close, he's on the short side.

"It's Nick," he says, giving Marnie a look. "Hey, you're Libby, right?"

How does everyone know who I am?

"Yeah."

Nicky—Nick—clears his throat. "Cool." He gives me a small smile.

Oh no, there it is. I'm a nerd magnet. No idea why. I'm not a gamer. Is it the copy of *Salt Kisses* peeking out of my knapsack? I push it down, mortified, praying no one saw. *Must convert to Kindle. Must convert to Kindle.*

Nick stays a minute, like he's waiting for something, but I just sip my sugar-packed coffee (that's how they serve it, thank God) and stare out the window.

Not today, buddy.

I spent junior high being teased after some of the boys on the wrestling team noticed Joshua Cades's doodles. "I love L.Z." covered his notebook. He was a shy boy who sat behind me in two different periods and was two feet shorter than me. "I love L.Z." began popping up on his textbook covers, scratched into his water bottle, marked on his locker door. It was a nightmare. As Libby Zimmerman, I was the only "L.Z." The jocks were relentless.

By ninth grade, the pool was bigger. I kept trying to start over as someone new, someone cool, someone like my sister. *How did she do it?* Sometimes Ver would let me raid her closet. That was how she was sisterly. But stylish outfits can only do so much. My default was invisibility, so save for a couple of friends, I just moved with the herd.

It was the only way to survive junior high. I'm a year older, and this isn't even high school. It's a little Podunk beach town in Maine.

I'm the new girl from New York City with an air of mystery. Maybe I can finally break out. I turn back to see that Nick has walked away, and he's ringing someone up.

Marnie stares at me, giving me that "reading" look again. Her lips are pursed. *Will she ever put down her eyebrows?* I squirm in my chair.

Marnie and I take the sidewalk from town until it disappears into one skinny road surrounded by huge gray rocks, a strait leading up to the inn and lighthouse.

"Our school's out early. Like yours, I guess," Marnie says.

"I do online school." My parents pulled me out after Veronica died.

"Oh, that's cool."

I look up at the torch, a flash in the lighthouse tower, then . . . gone. It's passed over to the other side and will circle around again. Is there some switch to keep it on? No one needs it anymore.

I focus, waiting for the light to return. Just as the light comes sweeping back, something else appears. A shadow. It doesn't belong. And then the light washes it away. I gasp, and Marnie turns to look at me. I try to pretend I haven't made a sound.

"What is it?" She looks up at the lighthouse, then back at me.

I suck the rough, salty air into my nostrils, clearing my head. "Nothing."

"Are you looking for something?"

"No. What? No." I try to pull my eyes away, but I have to look again. I have to see nothing this time. The light has just passed and is twisting around, coming back.

There it is again, the shape of a person, but pale now. Like part of the light. My skin prickles.

"Sure you aren't looking for the ghost?"

I turn to her, and she's grinning.

"Lighthouse Lizzy. Elizabeth. Wait—Libby—you're an Elizabeth too, huh? Ooohhh-oohh." She wiggles her fingers at me in a creepy-crawly way.

I just stare at Marnie, waiting.

She drops her hands to her sides. "Okay. Fine. She's the ghost in the lighthouse. People have seen her for years."

My jaw opens involuntarily. "What? Stop it" is all I can get out.

Marnie flashes that half smile. "Yep. I mean, not me. But other people. Let's see. Who's around now that's seen her? Jim Beam."

I raise my eyebrows. "Jim Beam?"

"I think he gave himself that name. He sells fake acid to the kids of Connecticut doctors and lawyers who summer here. Probably not a reliable source. An-y-way..."

She ignores my eyeroll.

"Oh yeah. Sharon."

Of course my aunt sees ghosts. *Live, laugh, and be haunted.*

"You're just messing with me. The light was blinding. Shadows up there could look like anything. Or you've got a friend up there trying to scare people." *Yeah, Libby, some girl just chills on the lighthouse deck, popping up every few minutes like a spooky jack-in-the-box.*

"So you *did* see her." Now Marnie's grin has faded. She gives me an assessing look.

I stay silent, hoping she'll stop staring. We've paused just before the bridge over the island.

Honk! A BMW shoots past us, only to have to slow way down as the bridge narrows. It slides into the handicap space in front of the inn.

"You see that?" Marnie shakes her head. "New York license plates, too. Jerk."

A man with slick-backed hair jumps out, and his polished wife gingerly removes herself.

"Where's valet parking?" he shouts.

"I don't think they do that here," his wife replies.

I can't help but snicker with Marnie.

"Oh, sorry, Libby. You're from the City, aren't you?"

"Yeah, but I'm cool!" I want to say. Instead, I just nod.

"It's not everybody. I remember your parents. They're nice. And I remember your sister." She doesn't add anything, only lets her words fade into the surf.

Gulls squawk, battling over something the New York man dropped.

"Hey, Libby, do you want to go to a meeting with me tomorrow?"

"What? A meeting?"

Marnie clears her throat. "It's a support-group thing."

"Oh." I went to these grief groups back home. I hated them. So much crying. Nowhere to run.

"Think about it. I'll see you tonight?"

"What?" I keep looking up at the lighthouse tower, but only the light passes by.

"The lobster boil. You don't really have anything else to do. I'll see you there."

CHAPTER FOUR

"Mint tea?" Sharon shoves a frosty glass with a pink flamingo straw in my hand just as I duck in the door.

"Sure. Thanks."

The doctor and his wife are squeezed onto a rose-print loveseat, brochures of various local activities spread out on the coffee table before them.

"@Dish29 says she sent her crab soup back *twice*."

"I'm not pleased with their Zagat score either, hon. Sharon?" He looks up from his XXL smartphone.

My aunt is setting glasses of tea on coasters that say "Blessed."

"Thank you," the woman murmurs. "Is there sugar in this? Or stevia. I absolutely cannot have stevia."

"She can't have stevia," the man echoes, zooming into something on his phone.

"Nope. Only tea." Sharon gives me a look, like she's just told me a joke.

"Sharon?" the man repeats.

"Yes, Don?"

"You don't fix lunches for a picnic, do you?"

"No, but I can recommend several excellent restaurants which cater—"

"*Twelve* one-star reviews? How does a business like that survive here?" Don gasps, lost in his menu planning.

"May I take this upstairs?"

The couple looks up at me, startled.

Sharon smiles and nods. "I've got to change those sheets out. I'll follow you."

Ugh. No escape. I move up the stairs, Sharon behind me. I'm at the top when I realize she's been heaving a massive laundry basket and I didn't offer a finger.

"Oh. Sorry."

"This? You're fine!" She drops it with a *thud*. "Care to help?"

"Yeah. Sure." I set my glass on the hall table that holds the toaster, coffeepot, and mini fridge. A near-empty basket of bagels—probably from that café, I think it's actually just called *Greek Café*—and a couple of slices of coffee cake are what remain of the continental breakfast the inn offers.

"I would never run a bed-and-breakfast," Sharon says to me and the snack platters. "Breakfast with strangers? Planned activities—like people come to a rugged New England beach for that? Please. Even I need some space." And she winks at me.

Suddenly I get the feeling that there is more to Aunt Sharon than I had assumed.

"Would you like help unpacking?" Sharon gestures toward my new room down the hall.

No.

"Uh, sure," I say because I have no clue how to tell this lady no.

She follows me as I tug on the sticking white-painted door, pulling open the thin barrier between the guest side and the living side.

"Do you need shampoo, soap, anything?" she offers eagerly as I flip open my massive black suitcase, resigning myself to finally hanging clothes and laying down a few roots.

"I think I have everything . . ." I pull out two purses of toiletries, full of face masks and scrubs and eyelash curlers that my sister had left when she moved out last year.

"Do you like lavender?"

"I guess so."

"I love it! If you don't, just tell me. I hung a sachet to freshen your closet. It's so small. But you see this dresser—I put another sachet in the top drawer too—for your undergarments. I like my bras to smell like flowers." She chuckled. "But you'll tell me if it's too much?"

"That sounds fine." I'm setting Veronica's potions and primp machines in a row. I place them carefully along the shelf above the pedestal sink in the bathroom. Largest to smallest. I still don't know how to use them all properly, but I keep them anyway.

"Well." Sharon is hanging my black-and-charcoal wardrobe carefully. We work in the quiet. The memory of the figure at the top of the lighthouse flashes in my mind, but I don't know how to bring it up.

I lift my now emptied bags and push them under the high bed.

"There's a big dinner tonight. At the firehouse. You like lobster, I remember. Come with me and Frank."

"I like lobster" is all I can say.

Sharon accepts this as a yes.

"You always loved butter-soaked lobster. When you were little and visited, it was the only meat you would touch. You were so funny." She smiles, and a hint of that Marnie X-ray flits across her eyes. "Veronica wanted nothing to do with the stuff."

I nod in agreement.

"But you did. You loved lobster." She gives my shoulder a squeeze as she walks out, the scent of dried lavender floating just behind her.

CHAPTER FIVE

I try to take a nap but only sleep for a couple of minutes. I drag myself off my bed and attempt to get ready for the evening.

There's a *thud* at my door. I shake, jerking the chubby point of a black eyeliner pencil up my lid.

"Ow." I lick my finger and try to fix it, but it just smears. Another *thud*. Is that supposed to be a knock?

"Hello?" I call out.

Frank's voice answers. "We're heading out in five minutes."

"Okay. Thanks." *Am I supposed to still call him Uncle? Or just Frank?* I opt for nothing.

The window facing the lighthouse reflects in my mirror. I spy something on the sill.

My necklace. Again. I had left it on my bedside table. Again. The points of the star press into my throat when I sleep on my stomach, so I always take it off.

How? And who?

I rush to it expectantly, but it's just sitting there with no explanation. I'm met with a breeze blowing the white gauzy curtains from the window I'd opened that morning.

"I know."

The voice is so soft I could have missed it, but I don't. I look down two stories. The fire escape, the side of the porch, sprays of lavender. No one is there. I force myself to lift my gaze straight ahead.

It's there in the lighthouse. The shadow. She's watching.

My whole body shakes. *You're being crazy. More than usual. A ghost? A ghost who likes to play with your jewelry?*

I grab my necklace and fasten it at the back of my neck.

My stomach squirms and my hands shake. It takes me a minute to catch up with my body. I'm going to some big party —okay, it's at the firehouse with a bunch of old people probably, but Marnie's going, and her cousin, Nick, and probably the whole town, right? Nobody knows me. Sharon and Frank may know my dad well, but all they probably remember of me is that I like butter-soaked lobster and I used to have a breathing sister. That's it.

I pull on the liquid black liner over the top of my squiggly pencil outline. Veronica showed me that trick of tracing the liquid over the pencil to get a cleaner line, but I never can do it like she could. My eyes fill with tears, and I put the tiny paintbrush down. It's as if I can smell her, the way she smelled when she would fix my hair or do my makeup. Like bubblegum and cigarettes and fruity perfume.

Pills don't have a smell.

I knew what she was on when she still smoked pot. Once the smell had been identified by my mom during a confrontation, there was no missing it. And the sweet burn of alcohol on her breath had a distinct edge. But the more she grew as a dancer, the more she talked about things like "focus."

"I stopped that stuff, Libby. Aren't you glad?" she said to me during my first night at her tiny new apartment. I had been so excited. A sleepover with my big sister. Maybe now that she was out of the house, we could finally be friends.

"Yeah. So glad, Ver. That scared me," I confessed, looking down, wondering if bringing my ratty stuffed bear, Mr. Nubbles, was not a good move.

"Yep. Only at parties, now."

"Oh." So not really stopped then.

Veronica rolled her eyes at what I had not said. "Honestly, you're like Mom and Dad sometimes. It's the way things are. But I usually don't 'cause weed makes me foggy, and booze makes me fat." She laughed a tinny laugh. "No drowsy, chunky Rockettes allowed."

I nosed through her medicine cabinet later, like I did at everyone's house, as though it would give me clues to the mystery I was stuck in. Just stacks of the products that now grace my new bathroom.

I woke up on the futon in the middle of the night. I don't know what I had heard, but the next sound was like scattering beads and strings of cursing. I curled up and pretended to be asleep, my eyes just closed enough. I watched my sister on her hands and knees, picking white capsules off the ground, and dropping them into a little bottle. She must have left some in her hand, because through the blur of my squinting eyelids, I watched her clap her palm to her mouth. She followed it with something clear in a liquor bottle, something I had not seen anywhere in her pantry.

Liar.

A tapping at the door pulls me back.

"Libby! I have something for you."

"Oh. Come in."

Sharon opens the door, and she's draped in the most over-the-top velvet black cloak I've seen outside of Halloween.

"Look!"

"I see it." Then I realize she's holding something in her hands, pushing it toward me.

"Your dad and I used to play with this all the time. He mentioned you liked taking pictures."

"I do." Photography class was the only thing about high school I missed.

"Would you like to use it? Would you be willing to help me with something?" She pops open the top to reveal an '80s Polaroid camera.

"What do you need?" I've only used digital, mostly my phone camera. But I've barely even looked at my phone since I've been here. Social media seems so stupid and pointless to me now, and contact with the few friends I have, who don't even know how to talk to me anymore, is beyond depressing.

"I need you to take pictures of ghosts. Mwa-ha-ha!" Aunt Sharon throws her head back in a wild cackle.

"You're freaking the girl out, hon." Uncle Frank passes her in the hall without a glance in our direction.

"Oops. Am I?" Sharon immediately switches to serious. *How does she do that?* "For tourists. I take them up in the lighthouse, tell them about the ghost, and then they get their very own haunted lighthouse picture. See?" She yanks a life-sized black-and-white cardboard cutout of an old-timey woman with a formal dress and a bun piled atop her head into my doorway. The woman's face is pretty, young, and distant.

"Do you keep that thing in the lighthouse?" I blurt out.

"Yes."

My shoulders slide down in relief.

"Starting today. Just picked her up from the copy shop an hour ago. Isn't she great?"

Oh. My shoulders clench back up.

"Yeah. She's ... something."

"Oh no. Oh dear. Stupid!" Sharon hisses to herself, covering her mouth. "I didn't think. Sometimes, I just do not think, Libby! With everything you're going through and I'm laughing about ghosts. I'm so sorry. I was thinking it would be fun, but of course it's a terrible idea. I'll just get this outta here." She's wrestling with the gloomy cardboard cutout, and it appears to be winning.

"No, no, Sharon. Aunt Sharon. Sharon." *Jesus, what's wrong with us?* "It's fine. I would like to take the photos."

Sharon peeks earnestly from behind the beautiful dead lady. "Are you absolutely sure?"

"Absolutely. I like ghost stories." I try to smile. My mouth feels sore, like it can only muster a smirk.

"Really? We have a great selection in our little lending library downstairs. I can tell you all about Elizabeth. Are you sure this doesn't . . . hurt you?"

Everything hurts. "I think it'll be fun. Is that what the cloak's for?"

"This?" She seems to have forgotten she was wearing it. "It's for a little promo I'm doing tonight about the lighthouse tours. The haunted feature is new. It'll keep visitors excited, I think. So, if you like, you can have this." She hands me the boxy brown Polaroid. "I've got a big tub of film for it, so knock yourself out practicing."

"Thanks." I turn it over in my hands.

"Fra-ank! Oh, I didn't see you there. Sorry, hon."

I stay a few yards behind the pair of them as we lock up the home side of the inn, wave goodbye to the good doctor and his wife and the young family they are avoiding on the porch, and head toward town.

When the sun sets here, everything changes. The temperature drops. Wind picks up. Things soften. But that's almost everywhere. Here, it's something else, like the feeling when you're in an unlit room and you don't think you're alone. I turn to see the beacon, and it's dark at the lighthouse. Now it's made its way back, shining across the sky. And it's gone again.

A chill crawls up the nape of my neck. I feel eyes on me. I look at the group on the porch, but they're buried in their phones and children. It's not coming from there. It's coming from where I was just looking.

I squint my eyes, but it's either blindingly bright, or the moment the torch passes it's too dark to see.

"Sharon?" I catch up to them. "Do you have a maintenance person in that lighthouse? I mean, besides you? Someone who cleans or something?" I attempt to sound nonchalant.

Frank raises a grizzly eyebrow. Sharon rubs her hands together.

Apparently, my attempt failed.

"Why do you ask?" Sharon's voice gets a bit higher than normal.

"Oh. I just wondered. It seems like a lot to keep up."

"Well," Sharon replies slowly, "we have a man, a lighthouse engineer from Bright Point, come in every few months. The SBHS—Sayers Beach Historical Society—sees to that."

"I thought you were the president."

"I am. I mean the money for upkeep of the house. And Frank will replace an old nail or freshen up the sign at no charge." She gives Frank a peck on the cheek, and he actually looks embarrassed by the wildly romantic public gesture.

"Oh."

"But that's not what you really meant, was it?" Sharon asks, now facing forward again, holding hands with her husband. He's permitting it.

"Well" is all I've got.

"You wouldn't be the first person to see something strange in the lighthouse. Like I told you, it has a haunted history." Her tone shifts, lowering, crackling, darkening. She is using her narrator's voice.

Frank's shoulders are shaking a little.

"A hopeful bride, the sailor she had her sights on, and a dream turned to nightmare."

A strong gust of wind blows in, twirling our hair. I half expect to see some guy lurking with a giant fan, a special-effects master for Sharon's Ghost Walks.

"Captain James Estin was a dashing young man, new to the position aboard the *Persephone*, a gleaming trade ship. Its masts were gilded, sails like spun silk—"

Frank coughs.

"I'm still tweaking the details. Anyway, he was very, *very* good-looking. And quite fascinating, I think."

Sharon shoots Frank a look. He just smiles and shakes his head. I find myself closing in on the yards I had between us so I can better hear my aunt over the surf and chatter of beachgoers. We have walked along the parking lot and the sidewalk butting up to this part of the coast, and now we're behind a strip of shops and restaurants.

I notice a hanging sign: "Greek Café." Two figures are

coming out with boxes. I see Marnie first and wave, but she doesn't notice me. Nick does and flashes a smile, waving back. I glance away, my cheeks warming. *Did he think I was waving at him?*

Well, so what if he does, Libby? You're being polite.

Just don't want to give the kid the wrong idea.

"Hey, Libby!" I look back to see Marnie.

"Hey."

"See you at the firehouse. I'll save you a slab of baklava."

"Cool. Thanks."

"You want to go with them?" Frank has just used up his daily word quota to ask me this.

"No, that's okay. I'll see them there." I mean, they didn't ask me.

Aunt Sharon takes a big breath. "He met a girl named Elizabeth. Her father was keeper of the lighthouse. She was his only child, a known beauty, but lived an isolated life with her father here. She was a mystery among the townsfolk, and everyone assumed that the young captain was just as interested in the mystery as he was the maiden.

"Mystery and maiden—I like the sound of that. I'll stick with it. Anyhoo, Elizabeth's father had taught her himself after her mother died in childbirth. And when she turned sixteen, and other girls were batting their eyes for a ride in a fine carriage, he would not have her frittering away her time."

Sharon wiggles her fingers in the air at these words, and I notice she is wearing black lace gloves a la Stevie Nicks.

"No, he put her to work immediately, assisting him in the

lighthouse. He felt that if a woman could run a lighthouse, then she could run a household."

"When was this?" I ask.

"1900. Some of these shops were in existence. Your Greek Café"—*my Greek Café?*—"was once a house of ill repute."

"A what?"

"A brothel." She's actually shimmying her shoulders as she says this. "Or a bordello. Should I use the word bordello? It does sound a little more romantic."

"Um, sure."

"Romantic? With prostitutes?" Frank's laughing. You can't shut this guy up tonight.

"All right, fine. House of ill repute sounds intriguing, too. Like 'House of the Rising Sun.'"

"Great song." Frank nods.

"Yeah, great song."

He smiles at me. So I guess he and I will be able to talk about music. Or at least listen to it together to fill the awkward silence.

"So," Sharon continues, deep in character, "he took a shine to her, and she fell hopelessly in love with him. But soon there were whispers around the town about the captain and his interest in other ladies. *What's that? He's playing around?*" She's cupping her hands to her mouth, craning her neck from side to side, apparently acting out the various townspeople.

I'm trying hard not to laugh. It's like a totally new feeling, to contain a bit of joy.

Frank's eyes are twinkling. "Babe, we're almost there. Maybe a Cliff Notes version?"

"Ugh. It'll take all the flavor from it." Sharon throws her hands up. "Fine. The story goes that the handsome captain was out late with the ladies the night before he was to wed Elizabeth. He got cold feet. He brought his true love, the madam of the brothel—okay, that's an embellishment—and boarded the *Persephone* before dawn that morning. Legend says—I imagine—when the bride-to-be was dressed in her gown and on her way to the church, the townspeople all stared. They whispered—okay, okay, Frank. When she found out the truth, she was so devasted she locked herself up in the lighthouse and wouldn't leave. The night his ship returned, she put out the torch the moment she spotted the captain's boat on the horizon."

"How did she know it was his?"

"It was the largest boat that came to port here, and Captain James flew an enormous white flag with a red griffin on it—there's a photograph of it in the museum. So out went the lamp, and a storm blew in."

"A nor'easter can be very sudden and very violent," Frank adds, apparently the one detail of the story he feels is necessary. "If you were caught in one a hundred years ago, with no lighthouse pointing your way and these jagged rocks, you were finished." He points toward the shore, and I notice my uncle is missing the top of his index finger. It's a stub. *How did I never notice this?* It's not a huge thing, but still.

"The people of Sayers said they saw her that night.

Anyone looking out their window toward the lighthouse spotted a shadowy figure"—my skin prickles at this—"and suddenly the light was out."

I suck in my breath. They both notice. Sharon pauses once more, for effect.

"Then what?" I ask.

"Whadya think?" Frank asks.

"I think the ship crashed."

"It was shredded like a toy boat on the rocks. All the men on board drowned. Ten of them. Days later, the flag washed ashore. Elizabeth retrieved it, locked herself up in the tower, and died a week later."

There must be a hundred people here, and from the looks of it, most of them know each other. At the end of May, tourists are just beginning to edge into town. I follow Frank and Sharon and feel people looking at me again.

Oh, come on. I can't stick out that much.

Annoyed, I look to see who's staring. He's over by the lobster pots, surrounded by other firemen. He looks a little too young to be one, but he's got an SBFD baseball cap on. I watch him hoist a lobster cage over his head with one hand.

He looks like boys I went to school with. Boys that never talked to me unless it was to tease me about wannabe suitors like Joshua. I know his type. He's athletic and beautiful and a complete jerk.

And he won't stop staring at me.

A smile spreads across his face.

Blushing, I turn around. He must be looking at someone

he recognizes, someone just behind me, someone as beautiful as he is, but I only see a table of young families.

I glance back his way. An older man is handing him a pot, sending him through the doors of the VFW.

You're such a weirdo, Libby. Just stop. I scold myself in the way Veronica would have.

"Why don't you go sit with your friends?" Sharon asks, a little pointedly, I think.

Nick and Marnie are a few tables over, next to the lobster setup. Nick's cracking open boxes and setting out some kind of cake on the food table. Marnie glances my way and points to an empty seat.

I feel like a charity case, but there's no one else I know to sit with. I've got nowhere better to be.

"Hey, Libby." Nick offers a grin. I stretch my lips into something more than a sour pucker.

"Hey. What have you got there?"

"Baklava."

"Oh. Right. I think I've seen that before."

"Want some? I can get you a lobster plate and—"

"No. Thanks. I'm good."

Marnie's chatting with an older man who's chopping chunks of butter into little containers and plopping red hot crustaceans onto heavy-duty paper plates.

"Let me get you a plate." A deeper voice rings out to my left.

"I'm Ryan." There's that boy. And he's looking directly at me, smiling. His eyes are dark blue and his hair is light brown and all of his features look exactly like they're supposed to look on a boy pulled out of an outdoorsman magazine.

"Okay. Thanks."

My hands are shaking as I hold them out for a plate. I glance up.

"Want me to carry it for you?"

"Um " is all I get out.

He chuckles and walks over to the table with Marnie and Nick.

"You're Libby, right?"

For the first time, I'm not minding the celebrity.

"Yeah. I guess everyone knows."

"In this town? Yeah." He points at a group of kids who would never have sat with me in my school cafeteria.

"I'll be over there when I'm finished plating everybody. Say hey before you leave."

He nods to Marnie and Nick, who return surprised "hey"s. I detect more than a little edge to Marnie's response but opt to ignore it. I quietly eat my food and try to look like I'm listening to them, try to look like I've got something worthwhile in my own life, try to look as if I'm not hyperaware of all the eyes on me. Ryan is still staring, but it doesn't make me want to jump out of my skin like it does with the rest of the people in this town. It makes me feel nervous, sure, but pretty, too. A little bit special. When everyone starts leaving, he doesn't wait for me to find him.

*H*is hands are on my hips, his lips pressing against mine. Everything swirls in my brain. Is someone looking? The crowd has winnowed out. We're off to the side, under an eave.

I don't think Sharon and Frank can see . . . He tightens his grip, drawing me closer. Ryan pulls back, looking into my eyes. I brace, waiting for him to say something like, "You don't know how to kiss," but he just grins and kisses me again. I follow his every bend.

His wraps his hands around my arms. There's a bruise that won't quite heal, a place where I squeeze just above my elbows. It's where I hold myself when I think of my sister and what I should have done.

I quickly push the thought aside, but I've already begun wobbling. I want to reach around and comfort myself now, to keep myself from falling, but I can't.

Ryan has my arms.

"You okay?" He pauses, looking expectantly into my eyes. Breathing hard. He doesn't smell like I think he should, like wind and salt air and cable-knit sweaters. He reeks of garlic and lemon and sweat.

"Oh. Yeah, I'm fine." I yank myself away from the smell, from my sister, who will haunt every moment for all time. Just to prove my words, I wrap my hands around his face, pulling him in again, acting as if I know how to kiss him back, as if I've kissed a hundred guys, instead of just my neighbor, Patrick, on the bench in my apartment's courtyard. I act like my only kiss until now wasn't a desperate experiment to imagine what it felt like to have someone want me so much they could die from it.

He's obviously been kissed this way, and I'm not about to be forgotten in a sea of girls. I have a chance now. I can start everything over out here. I can—

"Walk with the dead!"

A clanging bell and a cry peels Ryan off my face.

A figure darts past us, draped in a black velvet cloak. "Hear ye, hear ye! Take a walk with the spirits tonight."

Aunt Sharon.

Ryan snickers. I can feel my face turn purple I'm blushing so hard.

"Hey, Ry!" Another guy who looks college age, also wearing an SBFD cap, calls to him.

"Gotta go." He smiles. "See you around?" He turns his

baseball cap forward again, gives me a peck on the cheek, and walks away.

"Yeah," I say a little too loudly. "Whatever. I mean, yeah." *Shut* up, *Libby.*

He turns back and flashes a smile. "Okay."

I'm staring as he walks off.

"Ah-hem."

"Oh. Hi, Marnie."

"Hey there. Good thing we didn't have to perform surgery. Dr. Crane probably hit the bars over an hour ago, and they're a few blocks away. No bars on Main Street. It's bad for the town aesthetic." She smirks.

"What? Surgery?"

"To get that thing removed from you. It was huge and getting really attached."

My face burns. How is she more "mom" than my actual mom?

"Marnie, aren't you supposed to be, like, seventeen? What happened to you?" I let the words loose, saying more to her than I've said to anyone in months.

She bursts out laughing. Like, *hard.*

I step back. This makes her laugh even harder.

Marnie links her arm in mine. "Come on."

"Uh. Sure."

I don't ask where we're going. I just take in the town for a minute.

Everything looks a little different than it used to, the way things change from how you saw them as a little kid.

Smaller.

The lights surrounding the arcade and bowling alley are half burned out. The bulbs circling the little Ferris wheel and lining the Scrambler in the adjacent gravel lot zing on their last gasp. They all look haunted in their own right.

There's an open play area with Skee-ball and racks of fluorescent T-shirts, the kind you see on every boardwalk. A guy that shouldn't be wearing the bright yellow mesh tank top he's got on chews on the end of a pen, staring at us from behind a cash register.

"Hey, Bill."

"Hey there, Marnie. Ticket machine can't take bills right now. Gotta get a few things fixed before the crowds."

A few?

"That's okay. We can't play tonight."

Thank God. I was imagining Marnie challenging me to air hockey, and it was just too depressing.

I notice a large glass box with a blue light shining on the upper torso of a gypsy mannequin. A sign reads "Carlotta Sees All." She's got her ring-encrusted plaster hands stretched out over a crystal ball. She's missing a couple of fingers.

This is starting to feel like one of those indie movies my dad used to make in college. My mom and I have to watch them every year on his birthday. He gives us the director's cut, and we pretend we care so we don't hurt his feelings.

"Seriously?" I ask aloud, staring at creepy Carlotta.

"Well, *now* you have to put a quarter in."

"I don't have change." Before I finish the sentence, Marnie produces a coin. She's much too easily amused.

"Uh. Thanks."

I drop it into the machine and push the button. It sticks.

"Sorry, ladies, her ink is out."

"What?" I turn to face Mesh Tank.

"The ink on the card. She prints out a card with your fortune, but you'll probably just get a blank."

The game plays what sounds like violin music, and I can hear the creaking as Carlotta slides her poor hands from side to side across the glass ball. The music garbles and her hands swing faster, faster than they should.

Marnie looks at me, then calls out, "Bill? I don't remember it being—"

The blue light starts flashing. The box shakes like a washing machine after someone's stuffed an oversized sleeping bag inside and spits a receipt onto the ground. The box goes dark.

"That was fun." I lean over to pick up the paper and toss it in the trash.

"What does it say?" Marnie asks.

"Nothing. Machine's broken, remember?"

Then I follow Marnie's gaze and look back at the paper, plain white a second ago. Words are beginning to reveal themselves, like invisible ink. A swirly, old-fashioned script in black.

I KNOW

I drop it like it's on fire.

I look at the gypsy mannequin. Did she always resemble my sister? Her eyes are wider, green. I thought they were brown. Her lips are almost-black plum. My mom hated that lipstick on Veronica.

"Where's my beautiful girl?" she would say. The pictures they kept around the house were of a freckled adolescent, a bit awkward, laughing in every photograph.

Before my sister's eyes were dark and empty windows.

Where's my beautiful girl? My mother sobbed the words out, holding my sister's lifeless body the day we found her.

The day I ignored her.

Veronica had stopped hiding her life from me. It must have become too difficult for her. Both of her roommates had abruptly moved out—she didn't say why, but I guessed it had something to do with her escalating drug use.

She put it in categories to make us both more comfortable. *Managing. Working. Resting.*

She had kept a steady gig tap dancing at a 1930s club off-Broadway. She also waited tables at a café next door. The jobs were supposed to fill in the gaps while she auditioned for her destiny. Veronica had received callbacks for several roles as a back-up dancer on Broadway, and she was just eighteen. We all knew any day she would get one of them, and then it would be a matter of time before she became a Rockette.

Rockettes were also a 1930s New York classic. A line of perfectly in-sync Barbie dolls. I'm not being fair. They are extremely talented dancers, and they do everything with perfect precision. My parents took her to her first show at

Radio City Music Hall, where the Rockettes perform, when my mom was pregnant with me. Veronica became obsessed at the age of four. She began taking dance lessons immediately after.

Everybody loved Veronica. Even me, despite how my parents showered her with praise and affection.

Especially me.

So I gave up on nagging her and pretended to believe, made myself believe, my sister when she said she had everything under control, that the pills were prescribed by a specialist, a dancer's doctor. That she was under a very tight schedule, and her agent had her going to rounds of auditions to get her in the door of her holy church, Radio City Music Hall.

She'd get careless after passing out the night before. When I'd visit her in her new place, I'd spy a half-drunk bottle and an open bag of weed near her bed, the pipe resting nearby.

"I have a system. I have to wake up at a certain time. I have to have energy—energy all day—do you know how much practice dancers have to go through?"

Yeah. I knew. When the dining room in our already cramped apartment was taken over by dancer's bags, piles of slippers and tap shoes, and the *thud* of feet moving in time, and we had to split up around the family room and galley kitchen to eat, it became clear that Veronica was not just the most important person *in* the family, she was more important *than* the family.

"I need your help. It can be tricky to maintain. I need my Libby." Veronica put her arm around me and gave me a squeeze. I soaked up the glow, drinking in the smell of Marlboros and fruity perfume. "Will you help me stay on track? It's only temporary. Auditions with the Rockettes open March eleventh. Once I nail that, I'll be on a set schedule. It'll actually be less work than I'm doing now, and I'll finally get some rest." Veronica smiled, and I remember thinking how she looked almost old. She was aging quicker than she was supposed to.

"What do you need me to do?"

Her smile washed the tired from her face. "Set an alarm on your phone. Three o'clock every day. Call me. Make sure I'm up for dancing at the club."

"What about your waitressing job?"

"They love me there. I can get away with missing a day if it happens." She looked away and took a small breath. "And if they fire me, it's okay. There are other jobs like that I can get. The dancing one in the evening is the most important. I have to keep it. I lose that, my agent will drop me. And if my agent drops me . . ."

No Rockettes. She didn't have to say it.

"Okay, so I should just call you at three every day? What about your alarm?"

"My system is delicate, Libby. All hands on deck." A small smile. "If I don't wake to my alarm, I will wake to your call. And if I don't wake to your call, you call Rudy." She texted me his contact info.

"Rudy?"

"He lives down the hall. He's kind of weird, but you don't need to hang out with him." She pursed her lips and I detected a small shiver. "He helps me out sometimes."

"Then I call Rudy and he'll wake you up?"

"Yes. He has a key."

I knew she wasn't going to tell me why. "Ver, what if he doesn't answer?"

"Worst-case scenario, you hop on a train and throw open the door and wake my ass up. My evening show doesn't begin until six. I have to be there at five for makeup and costume, so if you get to my place by four, it'll be fine. Your school gets out at two thirty, right?" She wasn't really asking. She had clearly worked this all out.

I nodded.

"Perfect. I knew I could depend on you, Libby-loo."

"Always." And I believed it.

"That's weird." Marnie stares at the paper in my shaking hands. "It usually says stuff like 'You'll find a man in far-off lands' or 'Beware of curses from dark-eyed strangers.' Then it prints your lucky numbers on the back. What's the matter? Why are you shaking?"

I turn the slip over, trying to steady my grip. "Oh. There you go. Two one one two. What's up, Libby?"

"Nothing." I jam the paper in my pocket, then rub my broken half star like a talisman, or a clue. Or maybe just to make sure it doesn't spontaneously combust on my chest. I look down to the half star, glowing electric green.

"Nothing you feel like talking about, I guess. Fair enough."

I walk alongside Marnie, headed to our original destination. She doesn't ask any more questions, and I don't ask where we're going. I'm busy clutching my necklace and wondering why those numbers bother me, too.

Then a memory flashes across my mind, a stretcher being pulled out of a dumpy building, the numbers painted above the door: 2112. A white sheet draped over my beautiful sister. My mother was screaming. My father was holding us both, shaking with sobs.

As quickly as she had raced through life, she had raced out.

Marnie and I are back in the rows of cottages. Everyone's got buoys hanging from their porches here. Marnie stops at the plainest one, the only one without boating props dangling from its rafters. Just a sign with a triangle inside of a circle nailed to the front door.

"Here we are."

"Are we?" It looks like a crack house. The neighbors must hate it.

"Yeah."

"Uh . . ." I'm thinking this is a place my sister would have snuck off to.

Marnie laughs. "It's cool. Come on."

I don't know why, but I follow her in.

We step into a kitchen, but there's no oven. No microwave, either. Just a coffeepot from what I see. It's brewing.

A group is gathered around something on the counter.

A boy who looks about twelve turns, an enormous jelly doughnut in his hand. He nods at me. Like a grown-up.

I clear my throat.

A voice chimes from down the hall. "Another successful walk. Two guests tonight! Do I smell doughnuts? Karen, you're wicked!"

Aunt Sharon. There's no escaping her.

Uncle Frank pulls up behind her. Sharon spots me, and I wait for something loud and embarrassing, but she just smiles.

"Don't keep her out too late, okay, Marnie?"

Frank gives me a nod that mirrors the boy's, and he and Sharon split and walk into separate rooms.

"Where are they going?"

"Their meetings," answers Marnie. I glance over to a display on a card table packed with leaflets and books.

"Signs You May Be an Alcoholic."

"Living with an Addict."

"When a Family Member Drinks Too Much."

I groan. "This is like *those* things. Twelve steps, right?"

"Yup."

My therapist told me to go to these, meetings for families of addicts. I avoided it by visiting the mandatory grief group. Now I feel trapped.

"Marnie, I don't have a problem. My sister had the problem." I can't believe I'm telling her this.

"You sound like a commercial. Come on, have some crappy coffee and a doughnut. You don't have to talk. Our meeting is for kids mostly our age. I'll talk. You can roll your eyes."

I sit anxiously next to Marnie. They've read through some stuff aloud, and now this older boy is talking, and I am just avoiding everyone's eyes.

"Yeah, so he's in the rooms again—over in the other meeting tonight."

Veronica never asked for help getting sober. She always tried herself. At least, I think she tried.

Weeks before she died, after we came to our little alarm agreement, I spotted what looked like a vacation brochure on our kitchen table. A girl was riding a horse along a beach, her arms outstretched toward the rising sun.

"Recovery *is* possible. Your best days are ahead of you at LiveWell Sobriety Center."

"Uh, Mom? What's this?"

My mom poked her head in from the next room. "Oh. I didn't mean to leave that there."

"What is this?"

She stepped all the way in and took a breath. "Your father and I were going to discuss it with her first."

"Her? Veronica? You're shipping her off to rehab?"

"Libby." My mom's voice shook. "We have to do

something. We can't make her do anything, but we can't support her anymore."

"What are you talking about? You're her parents. You *have* to support her." It was like I was talking to another family. Panic rose up, panic for my sister, for her once-in-a-lifetime chance at the Rockettes. If Mom and Dad had her locked up playing archery and doing trust falls or whatever, she would lose her shot.

I might lose Ver. I felt like I had just found her.

"We do support her. We support her dreams. My god, Libby, you think we haven't been supportive? But Aunt Sharon and Uncle Frank were telling your dad that we're not doing her any favors giving her money every month. She was slurring her words on the phone with me the other day."

"Aunt Sharon is crazy. You're crazy. She's finally getting her life together, Mom. You don't see her like I do." My mind raced. She would get it together, being a Rockette. She'd have to. She'd be responsible and happy. She just needed a chance. And I was going to give it to her. "Last time I stayed there, she went to bed early. It was really kind of boring. There was nothing weird. She hasn't done anything in six months."

My mom started to speak, and I cut her off. "Yeah, I believe her. Veronica's just tired is all. She's exhausted from working two jobs and worrying about this audition. Don't you want to see everything she has put into dancing pay off for her? Don't you want her to finally be happy?"

My mother wavered. I could see it in her eyes.

It was time to close it. "Two more weeks, Mom. Her

audition is March eleventh. That's like next Friday. Just give her a little time. If you don't see a change"—I held up the booklet to an image of girls laughing around a bonfire—"you can send her to camp." I grinned, and my mom returned it. Veronica was not exactly a s'mores builder.

I texted my sister after to give her a heads up.

OMG. I owe you huge, Libby-loo. I'm taking you out for your birthday Monday, just you and me.

I was giddy. I couldn't believe she'd even remembered. My birthday was only four days before her big audition. I knew I had made the right move covering for her. *Ver's already doing better.*

I'll meet you outside your school.

Where are we going?

I'm thinking about it. Somewhere special. It'll be a surprise.

Laughter breaks into my thoughts and brings me back to the meeting. The middle-school boy is talking about his dad. He's super relaxed. I'm super not.

"My mom said he couldn't stay unless he got sober. They got in a big fight. It was crazy. I left. Ate pizza over at Marnie's." He grinned as the crowd chuckled.

"I mean, of course I care. But it can't be too big of a thing right now. I can't get sucked into their stuff. They'll fight. I'll eat at whoever's."

"My mom buys warehouse cases of Snickers Ice Cream Bars, Justin. Heads up," a girl interjects. More laughter.

Well, that bit of happiness was unexpected.

Someone cries when they talk, and I stare at the floor. Someone talks about their older brother, and I throw up a little in the back of my throat.

Then Marnie speaks, and I dare to steal a few glances when she does.

"My mom's been sober for a year, and I'm grateful, but it's not about her."

What? People are nodding. *Of course it's about her mom.*

"I'd come here whether she was going to meetings or not. I need you guys." Her voice breaks, and I watch her fold and refold a meeting schedule that's probably meant for me.

"I need this. Because I can't be the person to fix her. I'm not in charge of her."

I shift in my seat, and it's noisier than I expect.

In the days following my sister's death, we cried. We were silent. No one ate much. In the weeks following, my parents tried to do the things you're supposed to do. They gave me space; they invited me to talk. They set up an appointment with a therapist "who's great. Just great, Libby."

The first couple sessions we chatted about books. She seemed like a strictly nonfiction type, but she acted like she was interested in hearing about what I read. It had been classics—*A Little Princess* and *The Secret Garden* were read to me constantly when I was little. Then I discovered Agatha Christie, and I pored through those books. I loved the puzzle of the mystery. I loved how sweet little old Miss Marple could solve a heinous crime over tea. I gasped whenever Hercule Poirot's "little gray cells" would unfold something totally unexpected.

I always skipped to the very end and read the last page first, because I don't do well with suspense. I know. I don't care. It's how I read.

And the murderers were often people that seemed nice enough, or maybe a little rude, but definitely not like the monsters they turned out to be.

In one therapy session, I spotted my reflection in a glass cabinet.

I looked small, folded in on myself. Shadowy.

I looked terrified.

I looked lonely.

I didn't look like someone that purposely ignored her sister when the alarm went off, when all her trust had been put in me. I was the girl who could be depended upon.

Reliable Libby. Predictable. Not like my sister. You never knew with her.

I attempted something with my hair the morning of my birthday. I tried my eyeliner the way Ver had shown me. When school let out, I said bye to Melinda and Drew. We were close in that we had been going to school together for the last couple of years, and we all liked reading and talking about it—Mel with high-fantasy stuff, Drew with comic books —and Melinda took photography with me. They had been over to my apartment a couple of times, and they had met Veronica. I was expecting them to be impressed that she was taking me somewhere exciting for my birthday. But they looked skeptical. I tried not to show how much it bugged me.

I'm out! I texted my sister, exclamation point and all. I was too excited to play it cool. My sister planning something for my fifteenth birthday was better than Chuck E. Cheese when I was five.

Even though I was already on my phone, scrolling through my feed (I rarely posted, but I liked following people's bookish and artsy photo accounts) I still checked my text messages every few minutes to see if I had missed a reply from Veronica. I did that every five minutes for the next hour, with a couple of calls in the middle.

My sister never apologized. I don't think she even remembered. I won't know for sure, because she died four days later.

Veronica's audition was Friday, March 11 at 5:15 p.m. I didn't forget. I had marked it on our giant family calendar a month before. I'd been doing a mental countdown for her the past month. I overheard my mom on the phone with her the day before, encouraging her. I didn't tell my parents about my sister's no-show. I didn't talk to Veronica after that. I ignored my alarms for her. After she blew me off on my birthday, I couldn't even pretend she gave a crap about me, so I did my best to stop counting the days, stop feeling butterflies in my chest, stop imagining the choreographers and directors giving my sister a standing ovation after her flawless try-out.

I had other ways to spend my Friday. At least this time.

I always walked home—school was only five blocks away —so I texted my parents that I was grabbing a treat with a friend first.

And I was. Trey bought me an enormous chocolate malt. The powder makes it better. He asked me questions about myself. He didn't pause for me to laugh at his jokes. Come to think of it, he really didn't make any jokes.

I had helped him with an English paper last semester. That was the only time he had spoken to me.

Now we were drinking shakes in the front window of a packed shop on the Lower East Side, and I was feeling pretty good about it. Fine, I was freaking giddy.

"So are you working on something for English?"

"Yeah. I wanted to talk with you about it."

My heart sank. *Of course that's why he took me here.* "Oh. Sure."

"You were so cool last time—I actually feel like I understand what I'm doing now."

"Thanks."

"I hadn't really thanked you."

"You said thanks."

"Yeah, but I owed you."

"This is it." I waved my hand. *Beep beep.* I glanced at my phone. *Check on Ver.*

"You okay? You need to be somewhere."

"Nope. Nowhere. What were we talking about?"

We didn't discuss anything important. Nothing earth-shattering, while my sister stayed in too deep a sleep because of her fog. Nothing of significance as the weed made her fuzzy on the amount of pills, and the pills made her fuzzy on the amount of booze. We didn't share any secrets of the universe while my sister choked on her vomit in her sleep. No diseases were cured by us when Veronica's last breath was suffocated, and her light snuffed out.

The therapist kept encouraging me to talk about my sister's death.

I was less enthusiastic.

There's talking and shuffling, and I look up to see that the meeting is over.

"You lived." Marnie smiles a little. "Want to meet my mom?"

No. "Sure."

Marnie's mom looks like she was cast for the role: a pretty, older copy of her daughter.

"Hi, Libby. We're glad you're here. In town and . . . everything." She offers Marnie's same partial smile, but her voice is softer.

Marnie said she was addicted to pills. I expected more of an edge. I expected a disconnect. I expected someone like my sister.

I guess everybody's different.

CHAPTER NINE

"Nicky. Like anyone's going to attack us in Sayers." Marnie admonishes her cousin, whose smile looks related to hers, except it's full. It just meets you and waits.

"See you at home, Libby." Frank nods again, giving me too hard of a pat on the back as he and Sharon walk past.

"There's lemon cake in the fridge if we're asleep when you get back," my aunt calls over her shoulder.

"Oh, I'll head back in a minute." I'm getting out of here as quickly as I can. No way I'm letting Marnie and her mom corner me and make me talk about my sister. No way I'm walking home with Nick. Nicky. *Where's Ryan?* I wonder who he's hanging out with. Not these people. Not in this place.

"I'm just keeping you company is all." Nick draws the words out. I realize this is part of their weekly ritual. He walks them home, and his cousin insists it's unnecessary.

"Okay, we'll take Libby home first, since we both live on this street."

Great. I'm going to get stuck in this thing with them, where we all stroll along together after sharing our feelings in a dingy room. I just won't answer any questions and maybe they'll leave me alone.

But Marnie doesn't ask me about anything. Her mom talks with Nick about his grandmother—her mom and Marnie's grandma, too—and how they just came back from visiting family in Greece.

I'm eavesdropping, because I do that, picking up scraps of chatter between Marnie pointing out the little cottage she shares with her mom (Dad is totally out of the picture). She works at the Greek Café while Marnie does housekeeping at the inn.

From behind me I hear, "Oh, Nicky, it was so powerful. I felt such an ancestral connection there. I brought back a giant tapestry of Icarus. And the biggest evil eye on my porch." I eye Marnie's house more carefully. It has its buoys, its hanging glass witch balls, but in between I see the dark-blue-and-white spheres.

A giant paper star hangs, lit, in the front window. I gently finger the broken metal one around my neck. My mother made it with her metal stamping kit. She gave it to Veronica before she moved out.

"It's the North Star." She laughed a little nervously. "It's to guide you. Light your way."

I watched her pause, then tie it around my sister's neck since Ver didn't protest.

"That's weird, Mom." Veronica glanced down, holding it to the light. It gleamed. There seemed to be waxy stripes across the points.

"I put heavy-duty glow paint on the star. See here. It will glow a bright green in the dark. Polaris—the North Star—was trusted by sailors to find their way. People have relied on it since ancient times."

Veronica didn't answer, just turned the charm in her sparkling purple fingertips.

"It's for luck," my mother said in a voice a little too light. It's only in my recollection that I can recognize the fear.

Ver placed it in her jewelry box. I played with the treasures in there when she wasn't around, since she usually wanted to be alone in her room.

She had only had it a few days. I was holding the necklace up to her window, the hot breeze blowing against the gauzy white curtains, the ever-present sounds of traffic like an urban tide below. She was out with a friend.

Something in my eyes stung. My sister was leaving, but she was never really there in the first place. I felt like I was in a haunted room, except the ghost lived and breathed, always out of reach.

It fell as if I threw it, but I swore I hadn't. The star hit the painted concrete floor and split cleanly down the center.

"I'm so sorry."

Ver had just opened the door as I picked up the two pieces. I cringed, waiting for her to flip out on me for being in her room in the first place, never mind breaking her jewelry. But no yell came.

"Oh, whatcha got there?" Her voice was hollow, her eyes unfocused, veiled like her windows with the curtains pulled.

Now I understand she was high.

She let me keep a piece of the broken star, like a scrap of connection. I wore that scrap always. Sometimes she put hers on. They glowed like alien stars in the darkness. Veronica's half disappeared somewhere along the way.

I never take mine off, except to sleep. I can't sleep with it on. I can't sleep with it off, either.

CHAPTER TEN

I'm up by myself, for the first time in the couple of weeks that I've been here, I feel like. I check my phone. A text from my dad.

JUST CHECKING IN, LOVE.

I send back a heart emoji. It's about all I do. Melinda and Drew message less and less. I don't blame them. They're on summer break, taking trips to the shore with their families, riding their bikes to the park, devouring giant ice cream cones at Ben's in Brooklyn.

Besides, I barely text back. When I have, it's only one or two words.

I throw on a Concrete Blonde shirt of my sister's and acid-washed short overalls that I am not sure I'm pulling off. I toss my hair up in a messy bun. Somehow, dressing up like her makes her a little bit alive, even if I feel mostly dead.

I walk into the main hallway and pour steaming coffee

from the carafe into a chipped yellow mug with a print of a windsurfer on the front.

I use up about a fourth of the cream and dump in two or three tablespoons of sugar. There.

Delicious.

The ocean is murmuring and the salty breeze pours in the open window.

This would probably be perfect if my life didn't suck.

"Morning." I greet Aunt Sharon and Uncle Frank in the private kitchen. They're both sitting at the table. Sharon has a big planner open, and she's placing about a million stickers in it to describe every detail of her week. Frank is reading a book I recognize from the table stocked with pamphlets and books at the meeting the other night. I guess this is their morning routine.

"First lighthouse tour of the season is at eleven. I booked a group from the ghost walk the other night. Care to help out? You can keep the cash from the photos."

My parents send Sharon money to give me every week, and I have barely spent it, but I'm thinking it won't hurt to build up some cash and blow it all on frappes and bagels or something. Plus, I literally have nothing else to do. My schoolwork is finished for the year. I don't want to look pathetic, following Marnie around—or worse, waiting for Ryan to invite me to hang out in an obvious way.

"Sure."

Sharon beams. She smiles at Frank, but he's busy nodding sagely and chuckling at something he read.

I have an hour before I'm scheduled to take pictures, so I figure I'll kill time at the Greek Café. Maybe Marnie will be there. Sharon mentioned she had the day off.

A chime sounds on the door, and once again it's as if I've got arms growing out of my head, the way people in Sayers stare at me.

"Be with you in a minute!" a voice calls from the back. I recognize it instantly. Nick leans out of the open door, spots me, and flashes a bright grin my direction.

I smile weakly and throw up a peace sign, which is not even a thing I do, but frankly I'm not sure what exactly *are* the things I do, anyway.

Nick walks up and gestures for me to follow him to a small booth in the back. He pulls a folded paper napkin with silverware out of his apron and sets it before me.

"You hungry?"

"Nah. Thanks." *Then why are you here, Libby?*

"Thirsty?"

"Maybe."

"I know what you need."

I can feel my face burning and have no clue why.

Nick gets to work behind the counter and, in minutes, returns with a frothy drink.

"Frappe." He slides it in front of me, then sits himself across the table. "I can take a break for a couple minutes."

"Oh. Cool."

I take a sip of the creamy coffee shake. "This is good."

"I knew you'd like it."

I try to smile back a little bigger this time. Maybe I wasn't being fair to Nicky-Nick-earlier. He's lanky and tan, with dark hair, and dark eyes, and man, they are really kind of beautiful.

What is my problem? Calm down, Libby, just because a guy is nice doesn't mean he's obsessed with you.

It's like I don't know how to just hang out with anybody.

"Well, I'm clearly interrupting something." A dusky voice breaks through, and Marnie slides in next to her cousin. I realize that I haven't stopped staring at him since I started sipping my drink.

"No, you're not," I say, way too quickly and way too loudly.

"Yeah, I think you are," Nick adds at the same time.

"Whatever." Marnie looks to each of us. Nick looks up at someone who's just walked in.

"Hey, Bill. Your usual?" He's out of the booth and back to work.

Marnie pours herself a cup of coffee and sits back down across from me.

"Whatcha doing today?"

"Helping my aunt with lighthouse tours. I'm taking pictures I guess."

"Cool." Her voice lowers. "Have you seen anything weird there since the other day?"

I shrug. "Hey, how long have my aunt and uncle been going to those meetings?"

"Nice avoidance." She crooks up part of her lips. "Years. They helped my mom. And me."

"Oh. But Frank was the one with the problem, right?"

"They both have problems. For some it's alcohol or drugs, for some it's their relationship with the addict. That's why we all have our own meetings." The way she's nodding at me, as if to include me in the "our" makes me shift uncomfortably in my seat.

I pull fragments from my mind of conversations between my mom and dad.

"I think I remember my parents talking about how my uncle used to be messed up. How he's totally different now. I don't really remember him being any other way." *Drunk* is what I mean.

Marnie nods. She takes a gulp from her mug. She's not saying anything else, and I get the feeling she's waiting on me.

I consider my aunt and her lacy, fingerless gloves.

"I'm not anything like Sharon," I say with a small laugh.

"You got that right," Marnie chuckles. "But why are you even making the comparison?"

"I don't—I don't know." Because my only reference for alcoholics and addicts and the people swallowed up by them are Frank and Sharon, and Veronica and me. My whole family, I guess.

Nobody knew where to stand when my sister was on stage.

Now that she's gone, there's just a spotlight on an empty space.

Except times like these, when it seems to shift toward me, and I just want to run behind a velvet theater curtain.

I wonder if Veronica ever felt like that?"

When she was always putting herself front and center, it didn't seem like she felt anything like I did.

I have a memory, a faint one, of her made-up face and gauzy dress, tap dancing her heart out.

She couldn't have been more than twelve. Even her awkward phase looked beautiful.

Veronica danced effortlessly. That was what hours of daily practice and bleeding, bandaged feet gave you. The appearance of perfect ease.

There was supposed to be a talent scout in the recital crowd that night. I was eight at the time, and I expected some guy in a top hat to throw a bouquet at her feet, scream, "I'm gonna make you a star!" and whisk her off to a candy palace somewhere.

I was a pretty young eight.

From the way she acted in the weeks leading up to the show, it seemed like she sort of thought the same thing.

As Ver moved in perfect time, I waited for the inevitable standing ovation.

Her face turned white. Her teeth were blinding in a frozen smile that suddenly appeared painful.

"Oh no," my mom murmured.

"Nobody noticed. It was a tiny misstep." My dad comforted her.

I hadn't seen any mistake. I only saw the slight change in her expression.

It was the first time I could remember my sister not receiving a standing ovation after a performance.

When we got home, she locked herself in her room and barely came out that weekend. She didn't eat, her eyes were red from crying, and the giant cluster of red roses my dad always gave her after performances sat like a crimson reminder on our dining-room table.

I couldn't understand. She looked great to me. Veronica always was the best.

It's now that I can glimpse the one thing my sister couldn't do.

Be average.

I stare into my frappe, avoiding Marnie. My eyes are filling with tears, and blinking as fast as I can isn't helping. It's pushing the little hot salt drops into my frozen coffee drink.

"I don't think my sister knew how to be okay."

"And you?"

"I used to know." I wipe my tears with the back of my hand. There's no hiding them now.

"Marnie?"

"Yeah?"

"I don't think I can be okay again."

Marnie's expression softens. She looks a little less intense, a little more understanding.

"You can. You will. Keep coming to meetings with me."

I nod. "I better be going. Gotta help my aunt with that tour."

CHAPTER ELEVEN

I spot a couple boys by the bridge of rocks leading to the peninsula. One of them is looking through a big container, one of them is checking his phone, and a third walks up carrying a fishing pole.

Ryan.

I stroll past their group, doing my best to look cool, unaware of their presence, and not like my stomach is doing jumping jacks.

"Hey!" a voice calls, and I turn to see Ryan setting his pole down and coming toward me.

"Oh, hey. I didn't see you. . ." I trail off, realizing how stupid I sound. *Really? I missed the group of three guys and their huddle of fishing equipment a few yards away on a small bridge?*

"What are you doing?"

"Heading back to help my aunt with a lighthouse tour."

"Cool, cool."

"What are you doing?"

"Going fishing. There's a pier at the other end of the block."

He steps closer to me. It's difficult to carry on a conversation.

"Wanna come?"

"Sure."

"Oh, sorry. You just said you're meeting your aunt, right?"

"Uh, yeah."

I don't know if Ryan's friends are watching, because his face is inches from mine, and I'm swallowed up.

"I'm glad I ran into you. I wanted to ask you something," he says.

Can he hear my heart? It's banging in my ears.

I don't completely mind the rock digging into my backside as he pushes through the space between us, his arms fencing me in, his lips pressing against mine.

"Ry." We both turn to see his friends impatiently waiting.

"Gotta go. Sorry."

"What did you want to ask me?" I blurt out, not sounding remotely casual.

"Want to go out on the boat next week? Tuesday?"

"Yeah, sure."

Ryan leans in and kisses me once more. "I'll see you later, Lucy. Libby," he quickly corrects, and I'm not sure if I visibly wince. "Libby," he emphasizes, picking up his fishing gear and heading down the road, giving me a smile over his shoulder.

I run past my aunt to grab my camera and follow her out just before the tour.

There's one woman from the ghost walk, and she's brought a few friends.

"She killed him on purpose?"

"So it would seem," Sharon says cryptically, even though there is nothing cryptic about her story.

"That's terrible."

"Yes, it is. Perhaps . . ." My aunt stares up at the lighthouse. The crowd follows her.

There's nothing there, but I guess she's going for dramatic effect.

"Perhaps that's why she paces the walk, why so many have seen glimpses of her, waiting. The light flickers. There's a clattering on the stairs." Sharon's speaking in a loud whisper, and the group of tourists strain to see and hear what she's describing.

We all follow her inside, packing into the small entrance at the base of the tower. It's a little larger than a shed, and it leads into the round base. I realize this is my first time going in. I have avoided it since I got here. I listen to Sharon rattle off facts as I resist looking up.

"The lighthouse was built in 1830, and they implemented the Fresnel lens in 1870. It projects the light farther and came into use in lighthouses up and down the coast."

Everyone murmurs, craning their necks upward.

"Of course, we can't see the top of the tower from inside. When you climb the last of the one hundred and fifty steps, we'll take a break on the platform, and then I have to open a small door that takes us into the lantern room."

Oh. So I won't see Lighthouse Lizzy looking down upon me. I dare to gaze upward. The spiral of black stairsteps stretching up the whitewashed brick tower is dizzying. It's full of light in the base, but the air still has this musty smell the sunshine won't clean out. I see Sharon's enormous cutout of the ghostly bride hasn't made it upstairs yet. She's propped against a table, staring my way. I back up and out the door.

"Libby? Are you coming up?"

"Uh, no, I just need some fresh air." And after that, I am still not climbing up to see who is waiting in the top of that tower. *Nope. Not ever.*

I wait outside the lighthouse. I close my eyes in the late-morning sun, listen to the rolling waves, breathe in the mist and salt. I feel a tingling on my chest. Instinctively, I grab my half-star necklace. It's like ice. Then like a hot coal. I let it go and slowly look up.

She's watching me. Not clear. Never clear. Just a little more than a shadow. Like a very faded photograph taken with a bright exposure.

Then she evaporates.

"See something?" A gravelly voice makes me jump way higher than I'd like to in front of another human being. Uncle Frank. He's come up with a wheelbarrow full of flat paving stones and squats beside a long wooden bench outside the tower. He begins laying the flat rocks in the clay earth surrounding the bench. "Of course you're on edge. Anybody would be. You've had a rotten year."

I nod.

"I wish we could have done something for Veronica. We tried."

I didn't. I *prevented* her getting help.

"She just couldn't see clear, your sister. Or she wouldn't."

I dare to look back up at the tower, my mouth dry.

Frank wipes his hands on his shorts and hikes them up before sitting on the weathered bench. "When someone dies like that, everyone blames themselves."

Why is this the one time that Frank decides to have a conversation with me? Can't he just regale me with stories of his youth spent painting lobster boats, slamming Budweiser, and rocking out to Led Zeppelin?

I pick up my bottle of water and take several gulps. It doesn't soothe my parched mouth and cracking throat.

I know why.

It's the words that I'm holding there. They want to bolt out of me, but I keep pressing them back. I feel like I've got a lightning storm on my tongue.

"Frank." Crap. One escaped. If I'm not careful, they'll all leap out.

"Yes?"

Stay back, I order myself. *What are you going to say? It is your fault your sister died?*

I might as well have killed her, like Elizabeth killed her captain. And that's why she haunts me, because she knows I'm like her. Maybe this will end in her killing me.

And I would deserve it.

I don't think saying any of that will go over well. I clear my throat and try to sweep away some of those cannonballs.

"Frank," I say again, collecting only the words I absolutely must use to release the valve of pressure building and keep it from exploding. "What if something could have been done?"

"What if"—my hands are wet with sweat as I fold my fingers together—"what if someone got in the way? Lied for her?"

"Someone?" Frank looks like he's got video footage of my whole life and has just watched it in fast-forward.

"Someone." That's the most, and least, I can say to keep from igniting altogether.

Frank turns from me, and he shields his eyes from the sun

as he looks where I was gazing a minute before. "She went as far as her lights could take her."

"Huh?"

"It's an old New England expression. My Presbyterian grandmother—your great-grandmother Mavis—used to say it about people that could stand some compassion. 'They went as far as their lights could take them.' People are flawed. They're afraid. And their sight is limited."

I'm staring at the tower, waiting to see her, but all I see is the passing torch. Then darkness. A pause. Light again.

What if someone stops watching when the brightness fades? What if they don't know it will come around again?

"Can you imagine lugging a thirty-pound can of oil up and down those steps?" The chatter of the visitors breaks through, and I tear away from this conversation and practically lunge at them.

"Okay, a little to the left." I back up a few steps, making sure to capture the full lighthouse with the two middle-aged women beneath.

Click. The Polaroid whirs out from the camera, and I tug. "One more." *Click.*

They each take about thirty seconds to develop. I'm no professional. My mom has shown me some things about lighting and angles, and I like taking pictures. But I'm working with an instant camera, not a multi-thousand-dollar camera, so I'm not sure what I can do with these.

Just try to get clear images where no one's eyes are red is the best I can hope for.

The photos are developing on the small wooden picnic table on one side of the path leading to the lighthouse.

"Huh," I hear one of the women say.

"Oh, that's so neat!" her friend coos. "How did you do that?"

I lean over the pictures. At first, I think they're still developing. Then I realize that the white shape in the top right is familiar, like it jumped from my eyes and into the photograph for everyone to see. The edges are a bit fuzzy, but there's no mistaking the outline of a woman, from the top of her bun, across her shimmering profile, down her torso. It's all you can see through the lighthouse window anyway. She's not shadowy in the photograph; she's bright, like the "mystical orbs" in the pictures Sharon showed off at the beginning of her tour. I had held back a snicker, because they looked just like sunspots, but Sharon was so enthusiastic that I kept my mouth shut.

Sharon has made her way over after bringing out the last pair of tourists. Her jaw practically drops to the table.

"Libby, how did you do that?"

Now everyone is staring at me. It's my new normal, and it's the worst.

"Oh, just—just a little technique with the sunlight and, you know, the positioning of the camera." Everyone is looking back up at the lighthouse tower now. They can't see anything. But I can. A gray fluttering. It's watching me. She's watching me. She won't leave me alone.

"Wow. How fun." The others ask me for pictures.

"Uh, sure."

"She charges twelve," Sharon says to the next couple as she groups them in front of the lighthouse.

"Um, Sharon?"

"For the ghost pictures." Sharon nods at me.

Well, I guess that's fair. Except that I have no idea how to reproduce the effect.

I clear my throat and tighten my ponytail. I lift the camera from the strap around my neck and press the open button.

"Here goes nothing."

Click. Whir. Pull. Click.

My glow necklace, my broken star, presses against my chest. Like someone's nudging it. I don't want to push her. If she wants to show up in these pictures, fine. Not my problem. If she doesn't, well, fan-freaking-tastic. Even better.

I think of the strip of paper the haunted electric gypsy spit out.

I KNOW.

What does Elizabeth want with me?

A confession?

My own neck?

I shiver again, feeling the star pushing harder against my chest.

The pictures have developed.

The second one has the white figure. So do the third, fourth, and fifth picture my aunt asked me to take.

The shape is on the balcony now, with one arm stretched out straight in front of her, her palm raised.

As if the spirit were pushing something.

I finally feel a release and dare to lift my charm. There's a red mark on my chest where the star was, like an ice burn.

There are eyes on me again.

I drop my chain quickly, hoping no one notices.

"That is really something," a man gushes, holding up the image. "I've got to post this." He's holding up his phone, taking a picture of the haunted Polaroid. "Care to share your secret?"

I force a smile. "If I told, it wouldn't be a secret."

There's still one pair of eyeballs on me, and they belong to my aunt.

"Yes, it really is something," she murmurs. The wind catches her hair, and she holds it from her face, keeping her gaze on me.

I have the sense to get away before Sharon floods me with questions. "I'm gonna go practice taking pictures." *Of anything but the lighthouse,* I think, like I can somehow cleanse the camera. Once my back is turned, I lift the half-star charm again. The mark has faded from purple-red to pink. It's almost unnoticeable.

It's the kind of thing that would make me feel crazier than normal, except that there are pictures—actual photographic proof—of the Lady of Death.

That was Sharon's most recent name for her, and it seems to be sticking.

The sky is overcast. The beach is pretty quiet. This small stretch of Sayers Beach is adjacent to the inn and the lighthouse and is only reachable by the rocky isthmus leading the way from town or by boat from the large hotel across the sea between the peninsula and the larger, busy beach.

This little bit of coastline is used by guests who stay at the inn and the occasional visitor who stumbles upon it after checking out the lighthouse.

A woman who checked in this morning is playing Frisbee with her corgi (there is one room on the lower level of the inn, with a separate entrance, that allows pets). She recognizes me and gives a friendly wave. I hold up my hand and quickly look busy with my camera, hoping she won't come over. She doesn't.

But someone else does.

"I saw you wearing that camera the other night."

I look up.

"Hey, Nicky."

He scrunches his mouth at the nickname. "Do you take pictures, Libby?"

"No, it's just how people from New York dress." I wince a little at how snarky I sound. I just don't want him to get the wrong idea. I have other plans this summer.

Like, maybe something with Ryan.

And not thinking about anything of meaning.

And avoiding Lighthouse Lizzy and her obsession with me.

And pretending I'm not consumed with the curse of my sister.

He gives me a side eye. "Do you want to be alone?"

"It's cool."

"What does that mean?"

"I mean whatever you want is fine."

He pulls his backpack off and unzips it. I peer over. He grins at my nosiness.

"You wanna see what's inside? I got no secrets."

"No. I mean, sure."

"You know, wearing a giant Polaroid actually seems like passable hipster style."

I can't help but smile. It totally is.

He's thumbing past a notebook and a bent paperback. *Ender's Game.* I haven't read it—too sci-fi. But I respect it.

Next is a black pouch, from which he unzips what appears to be a fancy, actually vintage, not 1987-vintage, camera.

"You take pictures with that?"

"Yes," he says simply, that shy smile creeping across his face. I quickly try to shut down the way it's making me feel.

Nick—*Nicky*—is adjusting the lens. He's moving a lever on the top. My mom would probably go nuts over his camera. I'd like to play with it myself.

"This is a camera Sharon had. I mean, I wouldn't normally use it or anything," I say defensively.

"I like Polaroids. Instant. Easy. Fun."

"That's true." I hold mine up to my eye and search out the woman throwing the Frisbee. The fat little corgi leaps up. *Click. Whir.*

"Can I see the picture?" He reaches out his hand. "I don't shake it. Just let it sit. Want to see mine?"

He hands the camera to me, and I take it gingerly. It looks almost as if a burst of powder and electricity is going to pop from it. It's a contraption of art, the kind of thing you would pay a shocking amount for in New York.

"Where did you get this?"

"My mom. It was her grandfather's." Of course. He didn't buy it. He's so utterly who he is. And he actually came here to take pictures alone. Veronica would want someone to find her on the beach with an antique camera and be impressed. She wouldn't even need to know how to take a shot.

I like knowing how to do things. And I want other people to know I know. So I'm a phony who cares, I guess.

"How do I use this? I've never worked with such an old camera before."

"It's a Kodak. 1940. Here. Move this while you look through the lens."

"It's really cool," I say. It is. I zoom in on a large rock with some kind of shorebird pecking at something with its long bill. *Click.* The button has a satisfying punch when I press down with my index finger.

"There you go."

"Where do you develop?"

"There's a photography classroom with a developing setup by the observatory. It's for the college the next town over, but they let anyone use it with their supervisors. And I go there a lot."

"An observatory?"

"Yeah. You know, to look at stars. Observe." He holds up the camera and moves along the horizon. I spot a fishing boat in the distance. *Click.* "I like getting shots of boats, fishermen.

The lighthouse has been photographed so much, but if I think I can get an unusual shot, I'll take it."

"Has anyone ever taken a very unusual picture of the lighthouse?"

He turns toward me with his camera. I smooth my hair anxiously, backing up a few steps.

Nick laughs.

"Behind you."

I turn to see the Sayers Lighthouse, tall and white, its top like a deep blue hat. The light from the afternoon sun is blowing out the white clouds to a brilliant glow, but there's gray rain clouds rushing toward them. They meet in the middle, worlds colliding above the tower.

I'm still blushing from my confusion before.

"I mean, you're unusual, too, Libby. I could take your picture."

"Shut up. Let's both get this shot and see how it turns out in different mediums." I squat beside him and open my Polaroid.

"You mean different cameras?"

"Mediums, cameras, whatever. My mom's an artist. Everything is a tool for creation to her."

"That's cool. To me, it's a tool for discovery." Nick puts down his camera and considers me. "What do you use things for?"

I lift my camera, knowing I've never seen Elizabeth on this side of the lighthouse. Dare her to stay away from my image and leave me alone. Beg her to tell me what she knows, even though I think I already have the answer. Terrified of her judgment and wondering why in the hell I am obsessed with the opinions of a jealous, murderous ghost from a hundred years ago. Maybe because I know her judgment is deserved. No matter what she has in store for me, it can't be worse than what I've got going on myself.

I pause and lift the lens to my eye. "Escape."

Click. Whir.

CHAPTER FOURTEEN

My lungs expand and the tightness in my throat releases. The days have strung together into the following Tuesday.

It's a mandarin sun dipping in the sky, and for the first time, it feels like summer. For a moment, I feel like the girl I've always longed to be, wrapped up in salt, sunglasses guarding my eyes, mattering.

Ryan squeezes my hand and then lets go. He's hoisting a cooler with one hand into the boat. The tall, lanky boy with him is untying the fishing net, tossing it on the dock.

"So you have a boat?" I ask.

"Yeah. I mean, it's my brother's. Just for a little fishing and screwing around."

The other boy begins tugging on the gas cord and releases it. I can't make out the name on the prow. It's too faded. Ryan had mentioned that they were all raised catching lobster, so it must have been a boat they all used.

I wonder if his brother knows he's taking it out. I don't ask.

I look back up to see the sky shifting in color. The boys aren't looking. "Is that . . . ?" I'm about to ask about the shadows overhead and stop myself. *Don't be a drag, Libby,* I tell myself in Veronica's singsong voice. *They know what they're doing.*

Into the boat we go, his friend adjusting something in the front, Ryan loosening the last of the rope and tossing it on the dock.

"Do you sail a lot?" I ask Ryan's friend, who's just introduced himself. David.

"When we can." David shrugs.

"Enough to know what we're doing. Relax." Ryan puts his arm around me.

We launch from the pier. A little water splashes on me, and I do my best to lean back and look like I'm not totally out of place here.

The boat rocks in metronome rhythm on the waves. The peninsula is no bigger than my arm. Ryan's friend pulls a beer out of the cooler, offering me one. I shake my head no, just slightly, as if I might say yes in a few minutes.

Ryan jams his hand in his back pocket, his other arm wrapped around me, and pulls out a baggy.

He's expertly rolling a joint. Veronica only smoked weed in front of me twice. The first time, I was twelve, and I lectured her. But I couldn't take more distance from my sister, so the second time, I kept my mouth shut. I hated the way she changed, the way the sometimes sweet, sometimes skunky smoke was another veil between us.

Usually my sister just downed pills in the bathroom when I was around so I could pretend things were different.

"Hey." Ryan kisses me, then hands me the joint.

"I'm good," I say, disappointed, and pass it to his friend, my fingers clumsy. David hands Ryan a beer, and he offers it to me. I shake my head. He cracks it open and starts drinking.

He kisses me again, this time pulling me onto his lap. I hate saying no, and I've already said it twice.

I feel like I have to say yes to something with him tonight.

His friend is busy on his third bottle, steering. "My girlfriend had to cancel last minute," David adds. "Looks like we brought more than we needed."

"Speak for yourself," Ryan replies, chuckling.

Ryan is finishing off his joint, and the peninsula is no bigger than my thumb now, the lighthouse the nail on it.

The waves are rolling like smooth boulders. I look around and suddenly feel very small.

The sun has dipped deep in the water, and the golden clouds have an eerie green tinge to them. The sky looks like it's slowly filling with smoke. The wind becomes persistent. Ryan doesn't seem to notice as he's focused on kissing me.

I belong here, now, with him, on this boat.

"Hey, which way is Sayers?" a thick voice asks.

Ryan's friend has set down his bottle. He's got both hands

wrapped around the wheel, and he's staring at the navigation screen that looks like it's from the seventies.

Come to think of it, the boat looks old.

"It's that way." Ryan points straight ahead, where I had been looking minutes before when I last saw the lighthouse.

"I don't know, Ry." The boy bites his lip, stretching his palm across his brow as if to shade his eyes, but there's no more sunlight. The smoky sky is turning black, and the wind is picking up speed.

It's carrying rain with it.

I lean over to hold a bar for support, and the boat lifts on one end, tipping back. I lose my grip, sliding and banging against the other end. Pulling myself up quickly, my shirt catches on a hook. I don't realize it until I'm pushing forward and boomerang back. It would be funny if I weren't so sore from falling. If I weren't so scared. If my top hadn't torn completely down the front.

It's out of control now. The storm has swept the sky, and it's stirring all around. I reach for one of the life vests in the hold. The boat lurches, and I catch the corner of one to lift it out and pull it on. I turn to the boys, pointing for them to do the same.

Ryan's yelling, but the wind's screeching blocks out the sound.

"What?" I yell.

Ryan's pointing at what I guess is the call box.

David shakes his head and gestures for him to come over. Ryan begins frantically pressing buttons, holding up a speaker and yelling into it. A break in the howling gusts makes the problem clear: the radio is whistling, whirring, growling. It's static and spastic, and no voices are coming through.

We're lost in a storm, and we can't call for help.

I think of the gypsy machine, of the ghostly figure haunting my pictures. The gale screams. The boat rocks like a carnival ride coming off its hinges.

"Elizabeth. Elizabeth, please." I'm whispering even though the guys can't hear me above the storm. "If you're messing with the signal, please stop. Please." I look up at Ryan's face. It's white. I must look like I'm desperately praying. Then he leans over the bow and vomits.

"Hey! Hey!" A halo of light floats in the sheets of rain.

"Help!" I'm screaming with every bit of air in my lungs. David joins me, waving his arms wildly. Ryan's still puking overboard.

"We're here!" I cry out hoarsely. I have no idea what "here" means. The sheet of gray is a wall between us and the peninsula.

The ball of light grows brighter, and what looks like a larger, slightly newer version of our boat pulls into view. Two men in raincoats are on the edge, one holding up a high-powered lantern. I can't help but notice how the sight resembles a vintage cover from some early '90s Scholastic mystery, the kind of book I would have picked up with my mom in one of our flea-market hunts in the Garment District. I blink my eyes to try to see clearly.

Frank.

Now I'm flooded with embarrassment and relief.

Ryan, who's fully above deck now, stands at attention. Frank and the man with him toss a weight into our boat. He hitches it to tow it behind, while the three of us climb over and seat ourselves awkwardly on his fishing trawler.

"Didn't care to bother the Coast Guard. Woulda taken too long besides."

Ryan and David nod, speechless. I stare at my uncle.

"Heard you'd gone out. Knew the weather was turnin'. Shoulda asked me first." Frank gives me a look that shrinks me, that makes me think if I were younger and we were closer, I might get spanked.

It's an awkward night. The storm that had been so frightening grew worse after we were home. The old windowpanes rattled. There was a high-pitched whistling around the tiny peninsula. And the lamp of the lighthouse had that shadow again, that shape. Like smoke, but darker. Like thick, heavy fog.

I wake up to a knock at my door.

CHAPTER FIFTEEN

"Good morning, sunshine," Marnie's voice calls from the other side. "You're missing all the fun."

"Hold on." I rub my eyes, throw my pajama-clad legs over the high antique bedstead, and my feet hit the chilly floor.

I check my reflection in the mirror above the door. Humiliation. Yeah, that seems right.

I open the door to find Marnie wide eyed, her ponytail pulled sleekly back, a mug of coffee in each hand.

"How did you knock?"

"With my knee. You're welcome." She hands me a cup, and I move aside to invite her in.

I take a sip. It's loaded with cream and sugar. I feel slightly better.

"What's up?" I ask.

"Oh, no, no, no. You first."

"I don't want to talk about it. I do not know anything about sailing."

Marnie snorts. My memory of the night before comes flooding back, and I cringe.

"And nothing really happened—I mean with us. Me and Ryan. My top being off, that was just—"

Marnie almost shoots coffee out of her nose. "Do what?"

My face is hot. "My stupid shirt. It ripped. Like, off. I was so freaked out, I didn't realize how it looked until I unbuckled my life jacket when we reached the dock."

Marnie is spilling coffee, shaking with laughter. She sets the mug on my bedside table and rolls, cackling.

"No. It sucked. You should've seen Uncle Frank's expression."

Howling.

"Shut up." I resist the smile twitching at the edges of my lips.

"You mean"—she gasps for breath—"you mean after you almost died on the ocean with those douchebags, you had to face Frank *in your bra*?"

She's crying.

"Shut *up*." I throw a pillow at her. "I'm done talking about it."

Marnie holds up her hand. "Fine." She's still grinning. Then those eyes of hers grow bigger. "Now what do you think is going on downstairs?"

I hear excited chatter from beneath the floorboards.

"What is that?"

"Reporters." Marnie smiles.

"What? Because of me?"

"Yes. Pictures of you exposing yourself up and down the coast have hit the front pages."

"Oh. Shut up."

"No. They're here because of what *else* washed ashore last night."

Marnie stands up and walks to my window. She opens it, and the breeze carries in the salt and gulls' song. I follow her and look out.

There's a crowd gathered below, circling an area, held back by a cop.

Just past them, I see it.

A skeleton. Of a ship.

It's enormous, and its broken bones reach far across the stretch of sand, past the crowd.

The ice on the back of my neck answers the question before I can even ask it. I instinctively glance toward the lighthouse torch, but I see nothing. Just the lamp, moving as it should.

Without a word to Marnie, I throw on my flip-flops and run downstairs in my PJ pants and Black Rebel Motorcycle Club tee that still smells like Veronica.

Aunt Sharon's got her cloak on, and she's passing out lemon bars to a pair of reporters sitting on her couch, who are trying to look like they're not sinking slowly into the marshmallow cushions.

"Oh! Libby. This is my niece, Libby. Our talented

photographer. I'm sure you've all heard of her famous 'ghost pictures' by now."

Blank stares. No matter, she's fanning out Polaroids like a deck of cards. "Look. It's not just a glowing orb or something. It's Lighthouse Lizzie's actual *shape*." Sharon ignores the skeptical expression on the reporters' faces.

"Roomful of reporters?" I mutter under my breath, giving Marnie a sideways look.

"Hey. One of those guys is from Kennebunk, I think," Marnie says defensively, but I see her grin twitching.

"Ooooh," I whisper sarcastically.

A whistle blares. We all lean to look out the far edge of the big bay window behind the couch. It's the police officer, waving some kids back from the exposed ship.

"'Scuse me," Sharon says to the journalists, who are holding up my pictures to a pink vintage lamp on the end table.

"Come with me, girls." She opens the door, and Marnie and I bolt out behind her.

"Excuse me, John—I mean, Officer." Sharon corrects herself as the crowd turns, many of them familiar to me from the lobster boil. The cop tips his cap to my aunt.

"We need to clear everyone from here. This relic falls under the jurisdiction of the SBHS—the Sayers Beach Historical Society. We have to preserve it and explore its ramifications." Her cloak is billowing as she speaks, like she should be chanting incantations instead of pulling legal jargon out of her, I suspect, ass.

"Right. Okay, folks, this way."

The children groan. A few people hold out their phones for pictures before following the policemen across the rocky bridge to the main beach on the other side.

"You've just got to *sound* like you know what you're talking about." Sharon almost cackles, twirling her cloak, and we can't help laughing with her. It's just like a good part of Veronica, when she had fun with her performance.

"This is what I think it is?" I finally allow myself a long look at what's before me. As soon as I do, I grow clammy all over. I look back up at the lighthouse. Still just the turning beam.

I survey the limbs of the exposed ship, like buried treasure unearthed, and I know why I don't see her.

Elizabeth's not in the lighthouse because she's here.

She's all around me.

My muscles turn to ice as I hear whispers. I look around. Marnie and Sharon are roaming the debris. They don't hear anything. *Great.*

The whispering is broken, almost words. Not quite words.

"Oh my god, oh my god, oh my god." Marnie. I look up to see her bent over something. Nick—*Nick? When did he get here?*—has dropped his jaw to the sand. Sharon rushes over.

I stand frozen in place.

Marnie's brushing away rocks and sand. Nick has a shell, and he's digging beside her, pausing every few seconds to hold up his camera and take a picture. The whispering gets louder as they dig. *Does no one hear this?*

I glance around again. Then I realize the direction it's coming from. The sound is pouring from where the three of them are now crouched. It is louder to me than Marnie's endless "Oh my god" chant, louder than Sharon's squealing.

And now it's crisp, clear, and cutting through the air like the jagged rocks that tore through this boat long ago.

I know.

I know.

Then I see what they're shouting over. It's a freaking skull. And it's attached to the fragmented torso of a freaking skeleton.

I know, Libby.

Without another thought, I lean forward and vomit up last night's dinner.

"Isn't that . . . ?" Nick points to my throat. I grab it as if I have the power to make it go away.

"My mom copied it from an old pattern. She made this. She said she found an old design online. Very normal." But I hear my voice, and I most definitely do not sound normal.

The three of them nod slowly, as if they were trying not to make any sudden moves around me.

"Well," Sharon says with a smile that looks more like upside-down worry.

I head back to kick rocks over my vomit, careful to step around the poking ribcage curling up from underneath the sand.

"But why is *he* wearing it?" Marnie asks.

"I don't know. This is a mystery," Aunt Sharon replies.

My toe hits something. I squat down, assuming it's another wooden beam. It's not. It has that verdigris glow of rusted copper. For some reason, my mouth won't open. I wipe away the rocks and sand, glancing up to make sure the others are engrossed in their Mr. Bones situation. It's thin, flat, and wide. A box. A sealed box. I look up again. Nick's staring my way, so I offer a smile to reassure him. He returns it, and something warms the clammy, oppressive air that's been choking me.

"I need to get more film. And really, we should be getting images with our phones—do you have a good camera on yours, Sharon? Mine kinda sucks. Marnie's, too. She has the same model as me."

"Mine is pretty good. I left it back at the inn. Oops, I wonder if those reporters are still there."

While they're chattering, I nudge the box along with my foot. I slide it safely under a rock with a slight overhang. I'll come back to it later. Alone. I want to look without a crowd of prying eyes, especially my aunt's. I still cannot open my mouth to speak, and I'm fine with that, really.

I wouldn't have a clue what to say.

"Meeting tonight. Walk there with me?" The first remark isn't a question. I nod to both.

"Sure, Marnie."

"Five. There'll be pizza. We'll hang out beforehand."

Great.

"Okay. Sounds . . . okay."

Marnie flashes her grin, then bounds upstairs to collect laundry from the guest rooms.

There are more guests coming in. The house is getting full, and I'm happier than ever to return to my room and think.

What's in the box?

Why is the captain wearing Elizabeth's necklace?

I don't want to even ask myself the third question. The pendant tingles against my chest as the ghost of the thought sweeps across my mind.

My window is still open, the breeze from last night's storm cooling as the summer heat begins to curl in. I glance around my room. Everything seems in order.

Ever since she started showing up in my pictures, ever since she started really scaring the crap out of me, the spirit seems to have left my bedroom alone.

I lift my Polaroid out of my dresser drawer and lean out my window to get some shots of the unburied ship splayed across the beach like it's my diary ripped open.

Click. Whir. I pull out the photo.

Click. Whir. Another.

Now the lighthouse. Still nothing there.

Click. Whir. Pull.

The three pictures sit on my windowsill while I brush my teeth, getting the nasty taste of this morning's sick completely out of my mouth.

When I return to the window, I gulp in the fresh air. I feel the jagged edge of the metal charm, and tears pour out of my eyes, running down into my lips. The hot salt of crying is stirred by the cold salt of the sea.

I pick up the photos.

"What am I taking these for?" I whisper aloud, gulping in more air and tears.

"It's not like she's showing up in these pictures. Not the girl I need to see." My eyes blur and burn. "Not the one I need to forgive me." Now I can barely breathe. The salt is thicker than the air.

The first image develops, just the lighthouse, the beam

not visible. The other two take a bit longer.

One of them is fuzzy. Polaroids aren't exactly known for their crisp imagery, I guess. But as the remains of the ship come to light in the photograph, something I hadn't seen down there emerges. I recognize the glow instantly.

Elizabeth. The Polaroid feels electric in my hand when her name crosses my thoughts.

The figure is stooped over the wreckage, just as we were an hour before. Her arms are outstretched, and it almost mimics the way Sharon stood. Same place. Same gesture. Like she's holding the necklace. Polaris.

It was her, whispering. I knew it in my gut. But now I *know*. She must feel guilt. And she must be after me because I caused death just like she did.

She snuffed out the captain's saving light.

I ignored the alarm that was my sister's lifeline.

Maybe she wants me in this with her. Maybe she wants me to haunt the beaches of Sayers with her for eternity. Maybe she won't stop until I'm dead.

Because as this ice and salt swallows me up, it's as if I'm fading away.

"Are you all right?" Marnie's gaze bores through me when I meet her at the foot of the stairs.

"Yeah. Let's get to that meeting."

"I don't know why I even ask, Libby. You wouldn't tell me

the truth anyway."

This annoys me more than I like. I say nothing as we begin walking away from the house. I'm careful to avoid looking over at the wrecked boat.

"How crazy is that?" Marnie asks, reading my thoughts again.

"Crazy."

"I guess only a major storm could unearth it. Last night was pretty insane."

"That's what Frank was telling me. The wind. Only the most powerful wind and rainstorms cause that."

"Has he heard of revealed shipwrecks before?"

"Yeah. He said lots of missing ships around the world have been discovered like that. But . . ."

"But what?"

I allow her a peek into my head. "It's just weird that it would take this long for the ship to be found. That was like a hundred years ago."

I can feel her trying really hard not to drill into my mind with her gaze. I appreciate her effort.

"Very weird." She pauses. "Well, part of it washed up a few weeks after the wreck, I think. Some of the sailors' bodies. Other things. Like what's in the museum, right?"

We both smile at her use of the word "museum." The closet-sized room at the base of the lighthouse had a broken chair and a rotted steamer trunk on display, in addition to the photographs and a few writings of Elizabeth and the captain. Most of it was Sharon's embellishments and showmanship.

"Yeah." We're crossing the rock bridge now. I turn to look back.

"What?"

"You can't see the ship from this side of the bridge."

"No. You can't see most of that beach from here. That line of rocks is blocking it. And it slopes downhill."

"Huh."

"What are you thinking?"

"Just, if the ship had shown up before, people wouldn't know unless they were by the lighthouse."

"Oh my god. It could have been like this the morning after it crashed."

"Frank said that the records show two terrible storms that year, one after another. He thinks the boat crashed here the first morning, and then it was dragged out farther to sea, and buried in the next storm. He says the way it's coming out of the sand, almost like a fossil, means it's rooted there from a long time ago."

"I wonder if she found him in the wreck."

"I think so." I recall the image from my Polaroid and wrap my fingers around my charm. I can see Elizabeth in my mind's eye, hovering over the captain, reaching down. *Did she place the necklace on him?* That wet cold surrounds me despite the drifting June heat. Marnie is watching me carefully.

I look back toward Main Street and continue walking.

"Oh. So I guess we're done talking about this now." Marnie smirks. "Well, it was nice while it lasted. Maybe on the way home you'll tell me about more than your favorite color?"

"Shut up." I smile.

At the meeting, I head straight for the pizza and busy myself with a slice, avoiding eye contact. Then a second.

"Wow. You must be starving. Are you even stopping to breathe?" A girl I recognize from the last meeting laughs. She introduces herself and talks plenty, so I don't have to.

The meeting's a lot like the last one, except people are looking at me less. Some boy is talking about how grateful he is to have found this group, even though it means his dad is an addict, and I want to fling the rest of my cheesy pizza at him.

Then something happens. A boy who looks about ten, who was silent the last time, is speaking tonight. His dad's in the hospital. "He's on life support. My mom found him blue on the couch. I'm so scared. I'm so scared." He's sobbing.

My eyes burn and the tears begin to flow.

The boy starts talking about pouring out his dad's bottles when he was younger; then how it changed. How he started covering for him. "He said he was working on it. I didn't want my mom to leave him again. He was counting on me."

I can't breathe. I don't care if they all stare. I have to get out of here.

I grab my backpack and nearly fly out the door. I'm cruising down the front steps when I crash into Nick. *Right. Here to walk us home.*

"Whoa. Hey. Hey." Nick stays me with his hands around

my arms. "Libby?" he asks like he doesn't recognize me. Considering I'm showing emotion, he probably doesn't.

"I just can't do this. I can't. I can't." I'm taking in those gulps again, like I did this morning, but I'm farther from the beach now, and closer to the smell of stale tobacco and coffee.

Nick reaches his arms around me and holds me gently. He's stronger than I expected. I bury my face in his broad chest. Why did I originally see him like a kid? He's my age, and he's taller than me. And clearly more stable.

And he smells exactly like he should. Like salt and woodsy deodorant and sea air. I take deep breaths of him. I lift my chin, tears streaming down my face and painting my cheeks with mascara. He's hanging onto my every movement.

I kiss him like I've been waiting to do it my whole life.

I wrap myself up in him. I wrap my fingers around his face, and I wrap my lips in his.

My eyes are closed tight again, and in this moment I'm not feeling the ache in my heart at its full force. The volume in my head turns down.

And in the next moment, it cranks up again. "Libby"—he pulls back—"what are you doing?"

"What do mean? This is what you wanted." The words fall from my mouth as if totally separated from my brain.

"Yeah, but no. Not like this. Not like you are right now." Nick takes a step back. I must look a wreck, because all I see in his eyes is alarm. "You want to talk about what's going on?"

"No."

"I think you need to talk to somebody."

"I just want to let you kiss me." I lean into him again, stunned by my newfound boldness. This is the girl I ought to be. The girl from the City. The girl who can't be bothered to care.

"No."

"What's wrong with you?" I press as tightly against him as possible.

"What's wrong with *you?* You think you can just be like this with me? Just use me?" Nick pushes me away, cussing me out under his breath. I watch him pick up his camera. *Why did he bring it here? Was he going to take pictures?*

He slings it over his shoulder and fades into the darkness.

I storm off the other way, cutting straight along Main Street toward the inn.

There's a couple making out on the corner. The girl's giggling. The boy turns his head toward me and the streetlamp shines on his face.

Ryan.

You have got to be freaking kidding me.

I shove my hands in my pockets and practically run past them until I get to the bridge. Of course this is how my night is going. It's how my summer is going. It's how my life is going.

My phone beeps.

Hey, sweetie. Hope all is well. We love you.

Another text from my mom, in her valiant attempt to give me space. Sometimes, I wish she would just call me ten times in a row, so I could roll my eyes like Veronica while I ignored her.

Really, I wish my parents would just get on a plane because they miss me so much. Then I could turn them away in person.

Veronica did it all the time. I never saw a girl who was so beloved be so freaking unaffected by it.

But they are happy to give me space. Happy to have me away, safe in their artsy castle from the reminder of the child they loved and lost forever, the favorite one, the star of the show.

I respond. It's in my nature.

Love you too.

I don't have that ability my sister had. I can't even appeal to a geeky boy's hormones. What a freaking failure I am.

My phone beeps again just as I'm about to throw it. Marnie.

Where r u?

Feel sick. On my way home. See you tomorrow.

I'm off the bridge and halfway to the inn before she can ask more questions.

CHAPTER EIGHTEEN

I cry myself to sleep. I guess it's my thing now. I mumble, "Sleeping," when Sharon knocks on my door. I ignore the texts from Marnie. I'll pretend I rested off an upset stomach. They won't believe me, and we'll all keep dancing.

The light pours into my room, spilling over my pillowcase. I slide in and out of the fog of dreams.

I am putting on lipstick, chasing after somebody. Veronica is laughing at me. Marnie and Sharon whisper.

I run past them, reaching just ahead in the fog. I bump into Nick. He turns around, holding a book. I look at him, then look past him.

"Can I help you?"

"It's me. Libby. Wait—that's my book. *Maine's Haunted History*. What are you doing with that? Give it back." I reach for it, and he holds it away.

Something else takes my hand. Something cold. I yank my fingers back.

"No. My friend gave it to me. Who are you?" Nick stares at me blankly.

I can see it's my copy with the front cover bent.

"Give it back." A new voice—not mine. It hisses.

"No!" Nick and I both yell as something rips the book from his hands and swallows it in the fog.

Nick runs after it.

I feel an icy tap on my shoulder.

I turn to see a swirl of cloud, a puff of dust, and black.

Now I'm wide awake, and I have no clue how to feel, but I sense that idiotic is in the mix.

I know I shouldn't have done that to Nick. Maybe it was because I felt weird after the whole Ryan thing, which got impossibly worse on the way home. Maybe it's because I couldn't take what that kid was talking about last night in the meeting. Probably that. And something else. Something with Nick.

But mostly the first thing. And that's probably what pissed him off so much.

I check my phone. Nine. Museum opens at ten, and I'm supposed to be there for pictures.

I scarf down a muffin to avoid conversation with Sharon. Sharon pours extra cream in my cup. Without commenting, she's observed what a poser I was coming into town. I pretend I don't mind my coffee either way.

"Are you ready for pictures, Libby? Looks like you're feeling better from last night," she says after I've taken down the blueberry treat in three enormous bites.

"Yeah, much better. Thanks. Ready." I pat the Polaroid beside me. "Are we doing any pictures by the boat?" I ask, trying not to sound anxious.

"No, no. I've been keeping nearby historical societies at bay, not to mention the Kennebunk Museum and my friends down at the police station. No one knows there's a skeleton yet!" she squeaks.

"We are all a little disturbed at how excited you are by that." Frank pats her and goes back to whistling his tune.

"Sorry. Not sorry! Frank, I just got that song out of my head. Now you're at it again."

"Hey, Gordon Lightfoot was very underrated. He was a storyteller. Cheesy, but so was half the seventies."

"What song is that?" I ask.

"'The Wreck of the Edmund Fitzgerald.' It's about a shipwreck."

"Oh, that's why you've been whistling it all morning."

"I could switch to 'Brandy' again."

"Oh my god. I used to like that song. Until Frank got it stuck in my head during a renovation on the lighthouse's electricity."

"I know that song." I chime in with the chorus.

"Noooo." Sharon covers her ears. Frank and I share a grin.

"No, we'll just do a ten o' clock lighthouse-and-museum tour, and pictures in front as usual. Then I have a special project for us." Sharon rubs her hands together, and Frank bursts out laughing as my eyes widen in fear.

"Okay."

There's a small group, one of them staying at the inn, the others just taking a bus tour of lighthouses in the region. Sharon does her thing. The crowd gasps at the right places and spends the next half hour walking to the top with her and milling around the outside after the two seconds it took to get through the museum.

"All right, big smiles." *Click. Whir. Click. Whir.*

"Sometimes our guests find a little surprise from the Hag of Horrors herself." Sharon catches the expression on my face. "Too much?"

I nod ever so slightly.

The guests gather around while the images develop.

"Hmph." Sharon is clearly disappointed to see perfectly normal pictures of tourists in front of a lighthouse. No spooks.

"Maybe it's payback for the hag comment," I joke, but not really. I would never take the liberties with Elizabeth that my aunt does. Of course, that's partly because Sharon doesn't live with a ghost holding her secrets, tearing through her life, and probably setting the stage for her death. So.

"Keep us in mind for your next ghost walk. Every Friday and Saturday until September." The guests nod, looking slightly less impressed than before the Polaroids they paid ten dollars for, and shuffle off.

Sharon turns to me. "Are you ready?"

"Maybe?"

"You're ready. Come on. Marnie and Nick are meeting us."

"Nick?" I cringe and look to the sound of footsteps on gravel. They're already here.

"You look better, Libby," Marnie remarks.

"Thanks." I avoid looking at Nick, though he's got no issues staring at me. *Did he tell Marnie? God, I hope not.*

"Well, now that we're all here, I have an announcement to make."

"You found Elizabeth's skeleton." Nick smiles.

"Oh! I know. You are the long-lost descendant of the lady who ran the brothel." Marnie grins.

"No. And No." Sharon raises her fist, and dangling from it is the necklace from the captain's remains, the necklace I'm sure Elizabeth placed around his neck, the necklace that inconveniently matches my own.

I gasp seeing it in her hand. Everyone's eyes are on me again. *Shut up, Libby. Be cool. For once.*

I push my toes into the sand.

Sharon starts toward the little museum room in the base of the lighthouse, and Marnie follows close behind. I wait for Nick to go, so I can lag in the back, but he's not moving. Crap.

"I'm sorry." I blurt it out. Only way to do it.

"I know. But thanks."

"Want to hang out after this?"

"Depends. Can you handle yourself around me?"

I can feel my face turning from scarlet to grape purple.

"What?" I glance up to see him smirking at me. "I mean, shut up."

He laughs. The tightness around my chest begins to unravel.

"You two lovebirds coming?" Marnie calls out.

I shoot Nick an accusatory look, but he holds up his palms. "I didn't say a word."

We all squeeze into the room, and Sharon begins clearing brochures about the area off a small card table, then pulling it toward us.

"Will you get that picture, Libby?" I reach for the solemn image of Elizabeth. "Not that one, sweetie. The captain."

"What are we doing? What was your announcement?" Marnie asks.

Sharon puts her finger to her lips, even though there's no one else around. She pulls out a shoebox and breathlessly lifts the lid. We all lean in. She's clearly relishing this.

I see what looks like a fancy wine glass and a pile of cut-up papers.

"Will you open the drawer there?" She nods toward a small corner chest. I pull the wooden knob, and there's a red tablecloth and black taper candles on top. "Pull it all out, would you? And let's set the table."

Marnie and Nick and I stare quizzically, then get to work. Nick and Marnie unfurl the cloth. I set the picture of the captain on it, then the brass candelabra I found underneath the red fabric.

"Of course you have this. It looks like you lifted it from the set of *The Munsters*." I can't help but smile at how weird Sharon is. She's hard not to like.

Nick and Marnie snicker. I realize that it's rare I joke around them. I think I used to be kind of funny. Before my life ended.

As I'm placing the pitch-dark taper candles in the candelabra, Sharon begins emptying the contents of the shoebox.

Marnie groans.

The bits of paper are letters of the alphabet. There are cutouts of the words "Yes" and "No," too.

I point to the last one. "NO."

"YES." Sharon lifts the white paper word. "We are having a séance, and the good captain's invited!" She claps giddily.

My throat is closing in on itself.

"Why the captain?" Marnie asks. "Why not Elizabeth?"

"Because I'm not completely out of my mind."

"I'm glad you clarified." I stare at the table as she sets up the letters in a circle.

Sharon pulls a pack of matches out of her purse, and with a flick of her coral-polished fingertips, she begins lighting the candles and speaking in hushed tones.

Nick closes the door and shuts off the lights.

I'm standing in a cramped, musty room in the bottom of a haunted lighthouse, attending a séance for a ghost that was basically murdered, and I'm doing it next to the boy that rejected my advances last night.

This summer is going great.

"Oh, Captain," murmurs Sharon.

"My captain," Marnie whispers, snickering.

"Shhh. It's dangerous to not take this seriously. The spirits resent it," my aunt admonishes.

I'm taking it seriously enough, in that it's taking everything in me not to bolt out of this candlelit doom room.

"Sorry," Marnie whispers, and the candlelight crackles.

Someone sucks air in. Is it me?

"Captain"—Sharon lays the scrimshaw charm on the table—"we invite you, respectfully, to join us." I'm just now noticing that Sharon threw a black scarf over her head like a veil. *How does she think of this stuff? And why?*

"Your story has not been truly told. You have been overshadowed by the vindictive woman who took your life. We are ready to listen now."

Silence.

"Put your fingers on the glass, like this." Sharon flips over the wine glass and rests her fingertips gently on the edge. Nobody else follows her. She clears her throat.

"You know, Sir Arthur Conan Doyle held séances all the time," Sharon says pointedly to me.

"Sir Who?" Marnie asks.

"Sherlock, right?" Nick asks me.

"Yeah, he wrote Sherlock Holmes."

"Well." My aunt waves her arm as if to say "that settles it."

"It's what broke up his best friendship," I add softly.

"What do you mean?" Marnie asks.

Sharon doesn't like where this is heading and looks like she wishes she hadn't brought it up.

"His best friend was Houdini," I say.

"Harry Houdini?" Nick leans forward. "That's right, I think I knew that. I read his biography a couple years ago when I was . . . researching for a project."

"Liar." Marnie snorts. "Nick got a deck of playing cards and he was reeeeeally into being the David Blaine of our school."

It's hard to tell in the candlelight, but I think Nick is blushing as he glances my way. My cheeks warm. I grin from ear to ear despite everything in my cool-girl persona. Cute is cute, and picturing a ganglier, more awkward version of this tan, calm boy giving sorcery his very best is pretty freaking adorable to me.

"Anyway, Houdini was obsessed with busting up all the fake ghost whisperers that were getting big in the twentieth century, isn't that right, Libby?"

"That's right. Lots of liars taking people's money, pretending they could channel their dead kids and stuff. Houdini was out to prove them wrong. But Sir Arthur was really into it—he believed everything."

"And Houdini believed none of it. It's funny that the magician didn't believe in magic, and the guy who made up mysteries bought it all." Nick watches the candles drip.

"And why were they like that?" Sharon blurts out. We all

turn to face her. "I mean, why does it have to be that everything is real or everything is a lie?"

I clear my throat. Maybe I can get us out of this room without having to play Light as a Feather, Stiff as a Board or whatever the hell my aunt has in store. "You know, Houdini's wife held regular séances for him after he died. They had an agreed upon code word." I fold my arms across my chest and lean back.

"And?" Sharon and Marnie ask simultaneously. I bet Nick already knows the answer.

"And he never showed. After a decade, his wife finally proclaimed the afterlife a fantasy of mortals, a fraud." *So there. Maybe I'm just crazy and my old camera is just an old camera and I see stuff and of course my dead sister won't show because she's busy rotting away, decomposing into dust. She can't hate me, or worse, cease to love me, since she's nowhere.*

"Well, that's nonsense." Sharon's voice is no longer a whisper. "That's one of the most self-absorbed, pompous things I've ever heard."

"How so?"

"How so, Libby? If the deceased don't play by your rules, you get to declare them null and void? Every spiritual concept, every divinely inspired painting, preaching, prayer is junk because your weird, dead, carnival-act husband's spirit isn't spelling out "kimono," or whatever, when you wish he would?"

"I think the code word was believe," I say, more faintly now.

"Well, I don't need his validation, thanks."

"There are still questions about whether or not he did come through to somebody. And his wife never stopped trying," Nick adds.

"You know lots about this, Copperfield." I grin again.

Nick shakes his head, smiling.

"So she told everyone to give up on their faith while she held onto pieces of her own? I am not a fan of Mrs. Houdini." Sharon has won.

I can even feel myself nodding. Dammit. Fine.

"Now how about we get on with this?"

Everyone goes silent. No one knows what we're waiting for, but the air is thick with summer must and expectation.

Silence. Minutes pass. "Let's join hands," Sharon suggests.

I frantically wipe my palms on my shorts, accept my aunt's hand to my right, and reach toward Nick's at my left. *Just great.* Clammy hands and spastic vulnerability hangover from my come-on last night while I get possessed. *Fanfreakingtastic.*

Nick's hand is warm, and my palms begin sweating immediately. In fact, all of me starts to drip as the moments pass into minutes. The dank room has no air conditioning, and even Maine can get oppressive on a summer afternoon like this one. Plus, my whole ordeal of a life is suffocating in general.

"Someone else speak," Sharon murmurs. "Maybe he needs to know we are all interested in communicating with him. Especially after all that talk earlier."

"We are interested in hearing what you have to say,

Captain," Marnie repeats obediently, the smirk on her face betraying her.

"Yeah, we are ready," Nick says.

I can feel eyes on me. "You know, Libby, you *are* the one who's managed to get all those creepy pictures. And you stare at the lighthouse an awful lot," Marnie adds.

I shoot her a glare.

"You've noticed that too, Marnie?" Sharon asks. "Yes, you are definitely a person of interest, sweetie."

I'm not afraid to send some of that death stare my aunt's way either, but it has about as much impact as whatever remains of my antiperspirant from this morning.

I clear my throat and inadvertently yank my hand from Nick's, wiping it on the front of my blouse.

What can I do? Maybe the captain can stop her. Maybe he can protect me. "I am listening. I want to help." I'd like to clap my hand over my mouth as soon as I say it.

"Good girl." Sharon gives my hand a squeeze, and so does Nick. He took my hand back immediately, and I'm only slightly embarrassed to admit that something inside me lit up for a flash when he did.

The air gets darker, impossibly. The candle seems to burn brighter. It sounds as if our group takes in one collective breath and holds it.

And the dripping sweat I felt minutes before now feels like icicles crawling across my skin.

"What?" I gasp out loud.

"Place your fingers on the glass now!" Sharon barks a whisper. We obey.

My hands are shaking. Their hands are shaking. It's making the glass rattle.

I think that's what's making it rattle.

"Who's doing that?" Nick asks shakily.

"Stop it. You are," Marnie scoffs, but there's something in her voice. "Or Libby. Libby? Are you okay?" I'm mesmerized by the cloak of cold that has settled around me. It's been waiting, like an invitation sent long ago, and I've finally arrived.

The flames dance above the candelabra, reflecting, stretching, splintering across the upside-down glass.

The glass rocks from side to side.

"Libby—Libby? Are you doing this?" Sharon stares at me.

I shake my head, still not taking my eyes from the center of the table.

Then it begins to slide beneath our fingertips. It jerks to a tiny word on the right.

"No."

"No? No, Libby's not moving this?" Sharon asks.

It turns and pushes toward a letter.

"I."

"I? Captain, is it you?"

The glass slides back again to the first word.

"No."

The chill down my shoulders paralyzes my fingers, and I can't move.

But the glass does.

"I."

"Just wait," Marnie breathes. "Let's give it a second."

Again, it twists and jerks.

"No."

And again.

"I." And again.

"No."

My mouth goes dry.

"I. NO." Sharon repeats.

I know.

And then the breath we'd all been holding is sucked from the room. The candles flicker and go out.

CHAPTER NINETEEN

At first, I think it's someone dragging their chair back, but then I realize the sound is softer than that. It slides, it squeaks, it scratches. No one says a word in the near-pitch darkness.

Clink. Something drops to the ground and then slides as if it's being pulled along the floor. My eyes adjust, and a crack at the bottom of the door lets in a scrap of light. My charm burns cold and tingles on my beating chest. I stare at the table, patting the place where the captain's necklace had been. It's not there. It's being tugged along the floorboards, under the seam of the doorway, and out onto the beach.

"Did the necklace just . . . leave?" Nick finally asks. His voice sounds raspy.

My throat feels like it's never tasted water.

"Shh," Marnie whispers.

Sharon sits like a statue. It's the most still I've ever seen her. The seconds stretch into minutes. Finally, she speaks. "I think we should go see."

Ugh. Why? Let's just forget this whole thing happened.

I can already guess where it is. The three of them are at the door, like they're eager. Seriously, what's wrong with them?

The light has shifted since we've been in our Patrick Swayze-Whoopi fest. Clouds have shielded the beach from the sun. They reach across like a blanket. Like a warning.

I look down and see a line marked along the sand, forming a path. Sharon must see it, too, because she is marching toward the shipwreck, following it directly. We form a line behind her, like stupid teenage ducklings.

It is, of course, exactly where it was. Where Elizabeth wanted it to be. Everyone is shocked but me. I've been watching her lurking around here for days.

"Did he take it back?" Nick asks.

"She did," I say without thinking.

Sharon nods.

"Elizabeth?"

"Yes." My mouth clenches.

"But why? She killed him. Why would she put his necklace back on him?"

"That's the question, Nick." Sharon squints her eyes, standing over the heap of bones that I would swear was picked up at a party-supply store and planted here as a prank if I didn't know better.

I've had enough. Elizabeth's obviously pissed, and I'm already in her sights. No need to go looking for trouble.

"I need some rest." I guess it's obvious I want to be alone, because no one questions me as I turn and run to the house and upstairs to my bed, where I close my blinds and pretend I can actually go to sleep.

A couple of hours pass, when I open my creaky door, head downstairs, and ask Frank to borrow a tool. It's about time for me to take a look at the box I hid.

But I am not prepared to do that by myself.

I pass Marnie taking a bag of trash to the dumpster on my way out.

"Hey," I say, not looking to talk. I keep walking.

"I'm finished with my cleaning. Going home now. You walking to town?"

I pretend I can't hear her.

Marnie catches up. "Libby. Hey, Libby. Was she talking to you? In the room?"

"What?"

"She said, 'I. NO.' And I thought of that note from the gypsy machine."

I say nothing, wishing she'd trip on driftwood and break her leg and forget what she was talking about. Forget I ever sat in those meetings, or had a dead sister, or came to this crazy town.

I wish I could.

But I can't, so I say nothing.

"It is the same, isn't it? Elizabeth's trying to talk to you. Libby, you know I'm not like Sharon."

I have to smile at this. Dark, practical Marnie compared to my flighty, blonde, storytelling aunt.

"I mean, obviously. She's nuts. I love her, but she's loony. I'm not like you, either. Or Nick. I don't read mysteries, or the biographies of ghost hunters—you are so weird, by the way— I don't take artsy pictures or search for my feelings in the sky—"

"What?"

"Nick. He's really into constellations."

"Really?"

"Yep. Magic set two years ago, hanging out at the observatory last year. Huge dork."

"Yeah, that was clear when I first saw him." I say it more disdainfully than I mean to.

Marnie won't let it pass. "No, see, I'm saying it with love. Nick is a gem. A freaking treasure. And you know it. You probably knew it when he walked us home from our first meeting."

I knew it when he first gave me that shy smile in the diner, and it unraveled me. But no way I'm saying that to Marnie.

"Never mind. You're not looking for that. You're looking for the regular, popular one. The hot guy."

"Don't you want the hot guy to ask you to prom?" I repeat Veronica's old question aloud.

"Prom? What? Are you talking to yourself again, Libby?"

Again? Crap, I have got to be more aware.

"And no, for what it's worth. The hot guy? What about the nice guy? The guy who'll walk you home and take pictures with you and not use it to get in your pants? The guy who won't take advantage when you're melting down and throwing yourself at him, even though he's totally into you."

"He told." I stop in my tracks, furious.

"No. We saw. Out the window. It faces the front porch. You pretty much shut down the meeting."

Elizabeth, wrap your ghostly fingers around my ankles and pull me beneath the sand for all time.

"But that's not what I wanted to talk with you about." *Yes, Please. Anything else.* "What is with you and this ghost? I didn't even know stuff like this actually happened. The last time I was creeped out by someone's spooky story was when I was a kid at Camp Poatoan. I believed in my friendship-bracelet collection way more than I ever believed in ghosts. But you— you have some kind of thing with Elizabeth. Don't deny it." Marnie holds up a finger to stop my protest.

We walk in silence.

"Look, I didn't used to talk like this. About stuff. Honestly, I mean. Nicky says I was always outspoken, but not about things that mattered."

I watch her face. She's staring across Main Street as we walk along the rocky bridge.

"After my mom kept getting worse, it was like it was contagious. At first, I tried to be the grown-up. I helped out at the café when she was too hungover to show up. I was ten. My grandparents were happy to have me there, since they knew Mom wasn't right, but they didn't know how bad she was. She hid it. It was hard to keep up in school. And sometimes she'd get better, and I still just wanted to die. I wasn't better. So it wasn't really about her. Do you know what I mean?"

I look down, following the *thump* of my worn, stinky Converse as we walk.

"It *was* about her. You were a kid. Her kid. You shouldn't have had to work. You shouldn't have had to do any of that stuff."

"But I needed to be needed, Libby. I was sick like that."

"You were ten!"

"And so were you, when you started covering for your sister, I bet."

"I was twelve," I say softly.

"Ah. So it all went down really fast for you." Marnie puts her arm around me.

We stop walking. My eyes burn. I'm batting away tears.

"You want me to hold none of the blame, but I'm pretty certain you carry *all* of yours, Lib."

I turn my face from her.

"I saw when you left that meeting. Just when stuff got real, you bolted."

"I don't. I can't . . . My story is different."

"Everyone is different. We're all so horrible and special. Anyway, I'm here. And I think you really need to talk. Soon. I'm starting to get freaked out about the scary stuff following you. It seems to me that if you were honest about whatever's going on, Lighthouse Lizzy—or whoever—wouldn't have so much power over you."

"Thanks." We part ways at the street corner. She heads home, and I nervously make my way to the Greek Café.

"Um, frappe please? Iced?"

Nick smiles. God. I would be bothered by how much I like it, but I'm too distracted by how much I like it.

"Frappes are always iced. That's what it means. I'll make you an extra large."

"Thanks."

He hands me a tall, frosty chocolatey-looking drink. I take a sip. Strong and sweet. Perfect.

I sit awkwardly perched on the bar stool. Nick's bussing the table of a family that just left. The doorbell jingles. Another customer comes in.

I sip my frappe all the way down in ten minutes. Nick comes to clear it. "Can I get another? In a to-go cup?"

"Sure." He grins. "You know we make those with scoops of instant coffee mixed with cold water? Before we add cream and sugar. It's like the equivalent of four shots of espresso per cup."

"Oh."

"You need another one?"

"Yeah."

"You're gonna be interesting to be around."

He hands me the next one in a see-through plastic cup. "Um, Nick?"

"Uh-huh?" He's wiping the hand blender.

"When do you get off?"

"Twenty minutes ago."

"Oh. Sorry. Was I the reason you were staying? I don't mean, like, you were staying for *me*, but as a customer. I mean." *This is why I avoided talking my first few weeks here.*

"I knew you didn't need that second frappe."

I take a small breath, like a hiccup. "You want to come somewhere with me?"

Nick turns to face me, and I instinctively look away.

"Were you talking to me, Libby?"

"Yes." I force myself to look straight at him. His eyes are dark and hard to read, like Marnie's. But unlike her, he doesn't say everything he's thinking out loud.

"So." I shift uncomfortably in my seat. "Did you hear me?"

"I did."

"Um, you want to, then?"

"Depends." He folds his arms and leans back against the counter behind him. I have been dying inside for months, but in this moment, it's like I can feel my insides falling apart. Strangely, it's more alive than any sensation I've had.

"On what?" I tug my pendant. Habit. I glance away from him to give my eyes a break. He's definitely got that same laser-beam stare as his cousin.

"On whether or not you can keep your hands off me."

I'm dead. My face feels like it's on fire. I glance around to see if anyone's looking. It's late afternoon, and I realize there's only one other customer. He's busy with his paper, but I swear he's trying not to smile.

I turn back to Nick, who's got that mile-wide grin again. He's laughing. I'm glaring.

"Yeah. Let's go."

"Poppy, I'm off," he calls into a swinging door.

"Okay, Nicky. See you tomorrow."

"I gotta swing by my house first," he says as he opens the door. Old school.

We walk in the direction of his place.

There's a voice in my head telling me to be cool, to stay quiet. I ignore it. "Nick, I don't think I'm doing you a big favor. Hanging out like this. I'm kinda messed up."

"I noticed."

"I don't think you can fix me."

"Why do you think I'm here to fix you?"

"Because you're either broken or you're fixing somebody," I blurt out.

Nick is wide eyed. "Good thing you're going to those meetings. Might want to add a few in."

We reach his place, right by Marnie's. It's a faint blue. "Come in."

I follow him through the banging screen door. The house is small but open. It is scrubbed clean with glowing white walls. There are a few pictures up, and I can see straight to the kitchen, where the walls are lined with sparkling blue-and-white plates. The wooden floorboards look like they were worn down with sand. There's a woman at the kitchen sink. "Hi, Nicky!" she calls without looking.

"Hey, Mom." He walks ahead and kisses her cheek.

I stand in the front entrance, staring at a collection of shells on the mantel. "I brought a friend."

"Hello." I sound so small.

"Come here!" she calls to me cheerily. "Libby."

Everyone here knows me without introduction. It's like being a celebrity in the worst way. *Oh yeah, Sharon and Frank's niece. No, not that one. That's the one that died. Very sad. Drugs, of course. The little one. Quiet. Not as pretty. Lizzy? Libby.*

"Yeah. Yes." I try to return the smile. And she's hugging me. She smells like the house, like soap and sand and a hint of pine cleaner. Her hair is bundled up in a pile of black waves on her head.

Nick lives in a seashell with his mom, the mermaid.

"Would you like some coffee?"

Nick snorts and roams down the hall.

"Oh. No, thanks. I got this." I hold up my cup.

"Yum. I'm addicted to those in the summer. Nicky makes them better than I do."

Nick reappears in a different gray shirt and worn khaki shorts. "I don't like to smell like the diner. I have to change when I get off."

I nod.

"We're going out, Mom."

"Where?" the mermaid asks.

"Where?" Nick looks at me.

"The beach," I say. "By the lighthouse."

"Is Sharon going to let us see the boat soon?"

"I think so. She just wants to look things over."

"She wants more ghost research is what she wants." Mermaid Mom smiles, and her teeth are like pearls.

I return the grin.

"Nice meeting you, Libby. Come over anytime. I'm nice."

"I can tell," I answer without meaning to. Nice with something fierce behind it, just like I would expect from a mermaid.

I say nothing as we head toward the beach, and Nick seems perfectly comfortable. My silence feels thick and awkward; his seems easy.

"I wanted to show you something." I pull the box from beneath the rock.

"Is that from the ship?"

"Yeah."

I look around. It's clear.

The metal lid is beyond rusted and stuck fast as I try to pry it apart. I brought something for this. I pull a screwdriver I borrowed from Frank out of my back pocket. Frank looked curious when I asked him for it, but as usual, he didn't ask questions.

"Wait, you haven't opened it yet?"

"No."

"Why?"

Because I was terrified to open it alone. And because I figured I should share something with Nick besides an angst-driven romantic flip-out.

"I thought we could see it together. You like this kind of stuff, right?"

"Buried treasure from a hidden shipwreck? Sure."

"I don't think it's treasure."

"Me neither. But, yeah, it's cool. I'm in. Need help?" He pulls out a pocketknife, and together we shimmy the lid up.

It was sealed tight, and that's a good thing, because what I see inside looks like a roll of leather. I gingerly remove it, the leather soft in my hand. It smells like tobacco. I notice a pouch in the corner of the little box and open it. Tobacco. Stale and sweet. A shiny wooden pipe, perfectly preserved. A fountain pen. What looks like a stamp. I recognize it as a press for sealing wax, like they used to seal letters. I remove the contents of the box and lay them in my lap, my legs crossed.

"Let me see that." Nick points at the stamp.

I hand it to him, and he flips it over in the dim light. "I knew it."

The markings etched into it are more than familiar. A circle of stars surrounding a larger, nine-pointed one. One word beneath it. NORTH.

"What—what do you mean, you *knew*?" I ask, not sure I want his answer.

"I knew it had to be the captain's, and I knew it had to be connected to you. Don't you see that, Libby?"

"I don't know what I see."

"You see what you can handle, and you're not allowing for much."

"You don't know what I've seen," I say, images of my sister's body gliding on the stretcher like a gruesome Egyptian queen sailing past my mind.

"I've seen some stuff. I've carried Marnie's mom home. I . . ."

"What?"

"Has Marnie talked to you about that?"

"Yeah."

"Okay. Good. Then you know. Her mom could have died from alcohol poisoning. I rode with her to get her stomach pumped. I sat in the hospital with Marnie when we thought my aunt might be a vegetable."

"But she didn't die."

"Everyone around her did. You think you're the only one who feels pain?"

"I didn't say that."

"No, but you kinda act like it. Like no one else has permission to feel grief, like no one else has kept a secret that tore them up. Like you corner the market on Goth or something."

"Shut *up*." My eyes are burning again. I want to push him into the sand. Or lean my head against his shoulder and weep into his seashell-house smell.

I can't do either, so I just stroke the leather roll gently and begin unwinding the thin straps tied around it.

He doesn't seem to care about it. He sweeps my hair away from my face so that I can't hide behind it anymore.

"I know you're in pain. You don't have to keep everyone out to prove it. I know you were in pain before she died, too."

"What are you talking about?"

"How old were you when you were last here? Eight? Nine? I saw your sister."

How could anyone miss her?

"I saw you, too. The scavenger hunt. Do you remember that?"

Oh my god. There was a town scavenger hunt for the kids one night. We all broke off into teams. Veronica was definitely not a part of it. She was down by the waves, ruining other girls' summer romances effortlessly, just by being herself. "Were you on my team?"

"I recognized you the minute I saw you."

"After we lost halfway in, we spent the rest of the night collecting glow necklaces and tying them around ourselves. We ran around Main Street like we were Tron."

"You loaned me a book."

"*Are You There God? It's Me, Margaret.*" I gasp. "My Judy Blume."

"Yeah, I put it down a chapter in. Not for me."

"Um, why would I have loaned you that?"

"You went on and on about how great it was and how everybody should read it. You offered to give it to me for the summer, and get it back the next year. I didn't know it was gonna be about getting your period and bra shopping or whatever."

I start laughing so hard I'm cackling.

"Plus, you made me promise to give it back to you. I wanted to make sure you came back the next year."

I have an irresistible urge to kiss him, but I resist it.

"I can't believe you remembered me."

"I can't believe you forgot me."

In the fog of my memories, the only light has been Veronica, and she's blinding. It's hard to see much when she's there. Unless it's really, really good. I can place him, the narrow-faced, dark- haired boy who treated me like we were fast friends, who was the kind of person I wanted to be, easy and comfortable and laughing.

And then my family went back home and school started and I fell in line. My books, my sister's scorn, and looking for things I didn't know how I lost. We didn't return. My dad's work and my sister's dance began to suck up even our summers.

"I want my book back."

"I think after six years it's rightfully mine, but I'll give it to you. It's yours," he says softly, barely audible over the crashing sound of the tide pulling in.

I'm dizzy. *Focus, Libby.*

Unfurling the leather, I can see that it's a loose wrap, like a journal cover, but not attached to what's inside. And what's inside is a picture and what look like folded letters. The photograph is fuzzy, sepia, but immediately clear to me. And Nick.

"Whoa."

It's the captain. He's in his uniform. And beside him? Elizabeth. In a white dress. With a man in a preacher's collar beside them.

"That looks like—"

"A wedding picture. It's a wedding picture. What?" Nothing makes sense. I hand it to Nick, and pick up the faded papers. They're soft and have the tea-stained patina of old paper. The first one looks like it's in a woman's hand.

Captain John,

I received your note last night. Thank you for your concern. My health has been unsteady of late, but my father has me under excellent care. I should very much . . ."

The writing seemed to drag and scrawl at this point, like the pen was slipping, or like a child had taken it and attempted words.

"Can you tell what that says?" I point at the lines.

"Employ? Enjoy?"

"Oh. I think it's enjoy. 'Enjoy a walk along the . . .'?"

"Beach?"

"Yeah, that must be it."

I should very much enjoy another walk along the beach when I am in better spirits, which should be quite soon.

Sincerely,

Elizabeth

"So how did they get from that to this?" Nick points at the wedding photo. "I never heard about her being sick—not until after the captain died. And I've been hearing that story since birth."

"And wasn't that more about death by rage and broken-heartedness?"

"Yes. That kind of sickness."

I open the next paper.

John,

I never meant to hurt you when I told you I must pause and reflect on your proposal of marriage. You must know it is not an allusion to my feelings. I return your wishes, but I fear I may not be able to return your intentions. My father fears for my state, and God in His Heaven knows he may well be right.

I am not well, John, though in your company it may seem differently. I feel alive again with you. I feel like I should never fall again, never be possessed by this demon sickness. I finally understand what Poe meant when he said he "Loved with a love that was more than love."

I do love you. I love you with love that is more than the sum of its parts.

It is for this reason that I want nothing more than to be your bride, and it is for this reason that I fear I cannot be. You hold my heart.

Always,

Elizabeth

Again, the print is blurred, but it's not the handwriting. It's the tearstains that have painted the letters.

"Oh my god," I breathe.

"I had no idea this happened."

"This is more powerful than if she'd held onto a paperback he'd loaned her years ago," I joke and turn to look at Nick. Eyes. Burning into my soul. I can't take it. Back to the paper.

"Is that it?" Nick asks.

"No, there's another piece right here." I unfold it. It's not a letter. It's got large Old English style print and a seal stamped on it. It takes me a second.

"It's a wedding certificate."

"Is there anything else? Any other letters?"

I look in the box. Empty.

"So something happened between 'I can't' and 'I do.'" I pause, thinking. That tear-spotted letter revealed a woman struggling. Deeply in love. "It wouldn't have taken much. I feel like the captain could have shown up at her door with a bouquet and an optimistic attitude, and she would have practically skipped to the chapel with him."

"Yeah, it did seem like she was only saying no to spare him."

"And being the hero gets old fast," I murmur, looking to the sea.

"What's the date?" The letter's not dated.

"What's the date on the certificate?"

"Oh yeah, good call." I look, and it's at the bottom center, beneath their names. "June seventh. That's the day he set sail. Remember?"

"No. I haven't been obsessed with this story."

"Me either," I say defensively. Too loudly. "But it's in the town logs in the lighthouse museum. Sharon says the date at every tour."

"Why isn't a record of their wedding there?"

I study the certificate, and just below the date lies the answer. "By the City of Shrevesbury."

"They didn't get married here. Where's Shrevesbury?"

"It's in another county."

"That sounds like they eloped. Must have been a secret."

"And he set sail that day, and his ship wrecked two weeks later, so who would have known unless Elizabeth told them?"

"But why wouldn't she?"

"The lighthouse went out. Why would she do it on purpose if they were married?"

"I guess she really didn't want her dad to know they were getting hitched. Wasn't he really sick then? Isn't that why she was running the light?"

"Yes. He was bedridden with pneumonia for a few days, they think."

"They?"

"I don't know. The people who tell the stories. Sharon says 'they' a lot."

"I'm not sure she's the most reliable source on all this."

"Maybe not." We both chuckle.

"So it turns out that most of the stories about Lighthouse Lizzy were completely fabricated."

"And probably seventy-five percent by my aunt."

"But if Elizabeth was sick"—Nick considers—"why was she running the lighthouse?"

"I don't know. It was only a couple days he couldn't get up there. Maybe she was better then."

"Why would her dad have been so against her marrying if she was better? Something is weird here."

"Everything is weird here." I grab my pendant to try to stop the tingling-burning it likes to do on the regular now.

Nick notices and raises his eyebrows. "You should show this to your aunt."

"Yeah, I will. It's been a long day, though. I'll probably have to talk her out of holding another séance after she sees it." I feel in my pocket for my copy of the lighthouse key. "I'm gonna put it in here and explore it with her tomorrow." I place the box just inside the door at the base of the lighthouse, then close and lock it again.

"Cool. Are you wanting to go home and, like, nap or something?"

"No." I laugh.

Nick shrugs. "I dunno. You sound tired."

"I'm usually tired. I don't really sleep." I allow myself another peek at those searching eyes. It's as if they're sweeping the inside of my head. Like the lighthouse torch.

Nick looks to the horizon. The line between sea and sky has shifted from cobalt to sapphire as the evening creeps slowly in.

"Now I want to show you something."

ick loans me a bike. That's the best way to get to the observatory. It sits on the edge of town, straddling Sayers and Beacon. It's little, attached to a small library.

"Since it's Friday, it's open a little later," Nick says, checking his phone. "I think we've got thirty minutes."

"How long to get there?"

"Ten minutes. If you can ride okay."

"I can ride a bike."

"I don't know how girls in Manhattan get around. I thought you just walked and took the subway everywhere."

"Okay, that's true. But I can still ride a bike."

I climb on his mom's bicycle, which, thankfully, is a wide-tired beach cruiser. Turquoise green. A glow-in-the-dark fish sticker sits on the bell.

Ring-ring.

My star necklace glows in the darkness, all juiced up and charged from the sunshine earlier. I put my hand over it for a moment, as if I could hide it, as if I could hide myself from the ghosts, the ones who keep showing up, and the ones who, terrifyingly, stay far, far away.

But its glow persists, matching the fish sticker on the bell. There are only streetlights to mark our path on Nick's block. Once we hit a trail lining the coast, it's dark. The moon is a small sliver. The darker it gets, the more the stars shine.

We're riding past the busier part of the beach. People are laughing. There's a huddle of teenagers, probably kids Nick knows.

If Veronica were here, she'd be in the center of their circle. I glance their way, as if I could catch a glimpse.

Nick glides like a seabird on his bike, the fluorescence on his tires the only light besides the stars that can track him. We spin along the cracked sidewalk and turn off onto a small paved road. Trees hang over. They make a silvery arbor that reaches as far as I can see. It's getting darker.

The light only leads a few yards ahead.

"She went as far as her lights could take her." Frank's words stick around me like the smoky scent of lavender bushes rising up from the earth. I'm led by salt and musk and linen and sand. I'm led with no map, no guidepost, no light.

How far can you go when you're stumbling through the dark?

I see Nick slowing down. "Sorry, I'm not trying to leave you behind."

"I know. It's fine. Where do we go now?"

Nick points to the right, down an empty paved street. It's off the beach, and you can only see dunes, but the crashing of the waves is a steady chorus to the night wind.

Now I see a couple of porch lights. As we approach, the wide porch of what looks like it used to be an old boardinghouse comes into view. I follow the line of the house to the left and see a tower-like structure, shorter and wider than the Sayers Lighthouse, with a domed top.

"This is different."

Nick chuckles. "Yeah, I know it's a lot take in. Poor thing. I don't know of any famous observatories in New York, but—"

"I've never been in one. The closest I've come is the Natural History Museum Planetarium. But I'm guessing that's not the same."

"Seems like the one thing we've got on the City is this." He looks up at the sky, and I follow. It's black now, and it's as if a brilliant light shines behind a drape of velvet, and someone has poked a million holes through the fabric.

I've never seen so many stars in my life. I gasp. *Have I not looked up yet this summer?* Nick takes my hand, and I grab hold.

The door is unlocked. There's a guy who looks to be in his twenties sitting at the front desk, typing on his laptop. He glances up. "Hey, Nick."

I instinctively let go of his hand. The guy notices and smiles at Nick. "We're open for another twenty minutes."

"Cool. Thanks, Steve."

There's a wide staircase that moves up three flights. It cuts off at an angle at each flight, and we make a sharp turn to the next level, which opens to a large space. There's only starlight in this room. No one is here. I guess this is not the place to be on Friday nights, even for the students at the nearby college in Shrevesbury it serves. It's about three times the size of the lighthouse top with a long bookcase full of texts along one side and a shelf packed with ferns on another. In the center is a large telescope. It's not what I expect, but I'm used to everything being super new and supersized, so.

"Out here." Nick points. I like how, even when he's leading, he tells me where we're going.

We push through the double doors onto a small deck. It's got wide metal railings, and it only looks slightly more stable than the outer rim of the lighthouse.

There's another telescope here, smaller.

Nick squats down and peers though it. He tips it upward and turns a gear on the side.

"Is the North Star your favorite?"

"Um, I don't know. I don't have a favorite. It's just this thing I wear."

"Do you know what Polaris is about?"

"It's the guiding star, right?"

He nods. "Like the sailors used. It was crucial when you were way out at sea, before electronic navigation systems."

"Especially if the lighthouse was out."

"It could still just give you an idea of where to go. They had to use a bunch of tools."

"Yeah. A compass and the metal protractor thingy and aged maps that people like my parents pay a fortune to hang on their walls."

Nick grins. "Right. School's out. Look up there, and I can show you through the telescope. See that?" He points his finger to the brightest star.

"Is that Polaris?"

"No, that's Venus."

"Oh. That's right, I knew that. Where's Cassiopeia?" I'm trying to look like I know more than I do. The expression on his face tells me he's not buying it.

"This way. To the south, I think." Nick pulls out his phone and zooms in on a star chart. "This app shows the nightly location of all the constellations."

"That's not dorky at all."

"Right. I'm sure being brushed up on Sir Arthur Conan Doyle lands you prom queen every time."

"Shut up."

He grins in the darkness. I match it with ease.

"Here. Take a look." I lean forward, squinting my left eye and peering through the wide telescope with my right. It's black at first. Then everything comes into focus.

Crisp little stars making ancient pictures on their midnight paper.

"See how it kind of zigzags?" Nick asks.

"What? Oh yeah. Up and down triangles?"

"That's Cassiopeia. The crown."

"What's the story?"

"About the crown?" Nick asks.

"Cassiopeia is Greek, right? Aren't the stories rooted in Greece? Then the Romans started to see them in the stars?"

"Sort of. What, I'm Greek so I have to know all the myths?"

"No, you're a nerd so you have to know all the myths." I pause. "Like me. I know my kind."

"You just can't stop hitting on me, can you? Here's the short version: Vain queen. Bragged about her daughter's beauty. Got thrown into the sky by Poseidon for it."

"Harsh."

"Some of them are said to have gone there on purpose."

"The sky?"

"Like Ursa Major."

"Which one is that?"

"One of two bears. Ursa Major was the giant she-bear; Ursa Minor was the little one."

"Ah. Okay." I wish he would hold my hand. Wait, my palms are sweating. I wish he would grab me in his arms like one of those girls on the covers of my mom's books. I wish he would tell me I'm the most beautiful and fascinating girl he's ever known, and he'll absolutely die if I don't run away with him to live aboard a ghost ship.

Maybe that last part won't work, but that's the general idea.

He's not doing that, though. He's telling me about star bears that sound like me and my sister. I'm sure it's not intentional on his part. Unlike Veronica, I do not think everything is about me.

I usually think nothing is about me.

Except my disappeared sister and my broken parents.

That stuff's mine.

"Ursa Major is part of the Big Dipper, and Ursa Minor is part of Polaris. Check it out." He adjusts the telescope for me.

I look through, frantically wiping my hands on my shorts first. The air is getting chilly, but my hands can't tell, apparently.

"I see the Dipper, but nothing looks like a bear . . . is that square the head?"

"Some of them are a stretch. But can you imagine? They were trying to make sense of the strange world around them. They saw what they believed. There's another story about the big one—Ursa Major. From drawings on cave walls. Before the Greeks, people called it an elk."

"Yeah, really not seeing that either."

Nick laughs. "The elk was constantly running. It was being hunted, day and night. One night, it escaped."

"How?"

"Up there. Into the stars. Where no one could hunt it anymore."

I think of her. Of my sister. Like an elk jumping into orbit.

I hate her for it.

Leaving me here on Earth with all the hunters. Crap, I can feel the spear in my own hand.

"Seems like a cop-out." My voice wavers. "Why couldn't

she have fought back? Or gone to the herd for protection?" I know how weird I sound, arguing like I'm super butthurt about prehistoric doodles. Per usual, I don't know when to stop talking once I start.

I can feel Nick's eyes on me, that pressing family stare. He says, "Maybe she couldn't see that when she was running so fast."

"Maybe she could only see what was straight ahead." I stare at the points of stars, gleaming brilliantly. They start to swim together.

"Some people—I mean animals—are caged by their fear. They won't see other ways."

"They can only go as far as their lights will take them." I repeat Frank's words. I blink my eyes and let the constellations come into focus. The large scoop and the small scoop. "I'd like to look at Polaris again. Please."

I lean back. Nick moves forward, and a breeze ruffles his brown hair. It looks black in the dark. He's like a shadow come to life, a cutout of the sky searching its stories in a funny tube. I shiver.

"I wish I had thought to bring my hoodie—I'd give it to you."

"It's okay." I shiver again.

"This wind got cold quick. There might be a storm coming later." He takes his eyes off the telescope. Nick squints, looking out at the horizon. "I hope there are no boats out there."

I cringe inwardly, recalling the "incident." I hear Nick

snicker.

"Shut up. Oh crap."

"What?"

"Uncle Frank was going out for his sunset fishing. But that was a while ago. I'm sure he's back by now." I shrug off my uncertainty. Besides, it's just a little windy.

"He must be back. The sun set hours ago," Nick says. "Let's take another look at the North Star, and we'll head out."

He adjusts the ring on the outside, swinging the scope. Wind flutters across him again, carrying his smell in its sweep. Salt and cotton and . . . do eyelashes have a smell? What am I thinking? I'm thinking only of his scent, and the starlight, and the heavy web of lashes that thread his dark eyes. I don't care about my hands being clammy. They don't even feel clammy anymore. They feel electrified, wrapping around Nick as he leans over to kiss me carefully.

He's kissing me like he's unwrapping a present but is trying to preserve the paper.

I have never been kissed like this.

I clutch the fabric of his T-shirt and smell it. I don't know if he can tell. He's kissing the top of my head. My cheek. My ear. My eyelid.

He's not saying I'm the most fascinating woman he's ever met. He's not demanding I set sail with him. He's not saying a word, just pressing his lips gently on each available spot.

It's better than a book.

Crack!

A gust pushes us, and what sounds like the building splitting rings in my ear.

"Thunder. We have to go."

Nick grabs my hand and we run down the stairs. The desk clerk is coming out of the bathroom in a panic. "That sound was terrifying. Did you ride your bikes? I'd give you a ride, but I walked here."

"Let's just hurry." I turn on my phone to shoot off a text to Frank and Sharon, just to be safe.

My phone dings at the same time.

3 missed calls.

I CAN'T GET AHOLD OF YOUR UNCLE. HE WAS SUPPOSED TO BE BACK AN HOUR AGO.

Then my phone rings.

"I've been trying to get ahold of you for half an hour!"

"Sorry. I got your text. What do we do?"

"I don't know. I called Jim, he's local Coast Guard. And Sam. They're in contact with the county Coast Watch to get out there. I'm scared, Libby."

The fear in her voice is shaking me. "It's—it's okay. He is an experienced sailor. He knows what he's doing."

"So does the storm. If it comes quickly, experience means nothing."

"I'm on my way." I've hopped on my bike, and Nick is close by as I stay on the phone with my aunt.

"Wait, that's Jim. Hold on." Sharon clicks over for a minute. Then she returns. "They're gearing up. I'm going out with them."

"Aunt Sharon, are you—"

"I can't just sit here uselessly. I have to do something. Oh, Christ. Oh no."

"What? What is it?"

"I've got his meds. He left them in his other duffel bag and didn't switch them out. I was just going through it for the big flashlight, and here they are. Wait! Maybe he brought the other bottle." I can hear her panting.

"What meds?"

"Seizures. They're rare, but he gets 'em a few times a year —especially if he's stressed. He's been taking on way too many projects around here—that stupid gate and the deck. Why didn't he pay somebody like I told him?" I hear a creaking sound. I'm guessing it's the bathroom medicine cabinet. "Dangit, Frank! They're here. Oh, Libby. Oh, Libby."

"It's okay. It's gonna be okay."

I hear her draw a ragged breath. "Oh. Yes." She's obviously not focusing on me anymore, probably getting things together.

"What can we do?"

"We?"

"Me and Nick."

"Oh, that's right. You're with Nick. Are you okay? It's pouring rain!"

"The rain hasn't hit us yet. Must be on its way." And just as I finish the words, the once invisible cloud makes itself known by blocking out the stars overhead and pouring water over us like a set of giant buckets.

"Go home, baby! Nick, too. Keep him in our house until this passes."

"Are you sure that's all?"

"Yes, I'll feel better knowing you two are safe, at least."

"Lemme know as soon as you find Frank!" I'm shouting over the storm.

"There are blueberry muffins in the freezer! I'll leave them out to thaw!" Sharon's shouting too, even though she's inside the house.

Click.

We're fighting the sheets, plowing through the walls of water. Thank God I wore my Converse instead of my flip-flops. I can't make out a thing, but Nick seems to know we're heading the right way.

"Where are the lights? Aren't we in town?" The rain has turned down the volume a little bit, but the wind is picking up. We've made it to Main Street. It's like a ghost town. Every shop, every restaurant, every house is dark. I squint and make out a faint glow from a window. Candlelight.

"Power outage. Crap," Nick says.

"Across town?"

"Storm must've knocked out a transformer. This happened a few winters ago. Doesn't usually come with summer rains."

"But this is not a normal rain." The rain has softened to a mist, but the wind is whirling around us, making promises we don't understand.

"No, it's not." Nick picks up his phone. "Mom? I'm sorry. I

was trying to focus on the—yeah, I'm with Libby. Sharon's going after Frank. He didn't come back from fishing earlier. I know. I know. Yeah. I'm going to the inn with her. Are you all right? No power?" He pauses. "Do you need anything? Is Dad home? Cool. Okay. Okay. Bye."

We arrive at the rock bridge and hop off our bikes.

"Finally, a light." For the first time since coming here, I feel peace when I see the beacon of light turning. Relief washes over me like the rain shower. "That will help them all find their way back."

The front door opens. "There you are!" Marnie, like an extra mom, is tapping her foot, a crowd of guests peeping out behind her in their bathrobes, holding the flashlights that come in their nightstand drawers. It looks like the cover of a murder-mystery board game.

We run in, dripping wet, and towels are literally thrown at us from every direction.

"We were so worried!" A woman from Jersey whose name I can't place is tightly hugging me. Marnie grins, reveling in my discomfort.

"All right, everyone's home. Off to bed." Two guests actually groan but still obey her. They begin marching upstairs.

"You are the weirdest girl I've ever met." I shake my head, and I don't fight my smile.

Marnie snorts. "And *you* are the most *delusional.*" Nick chuckles. "And you spend all your time with us, so shut it."

He shrugs.

"You can borrow these. They're Frank's." Marnie hands her cousin a bundle of clothes. "It's a shirt and drawstring shorts, so you should be able to wear them without your pants falling off. You've got dry clothes in your closet, right, Libby?" She hands me a compact flashlight.

I nod and run upstairs, leaving puddles along the way.

Black T-shirt, jeans, and the XL sweatshirt Sharon gave me—"Leave the Light On!"—written like a vintage postcard with a cartoon ghost jumping from the Sayers Lighthouse and screaming. She ordered them weeks ago, and she's sold a few. On second thought, I fish out my hoodie crumpled beneath my bed. My flashlight is getting dim. Batteries must be dying.

I look in my bedside drawer, but I already know there isn't a flashlight there. This must be it. Oh well, I can make it downstairs in the dark if I have to. I throw off my wet clothes, pull on my dry ones. They smell like lavender dryer sheets. I squeeze some water from my hair with the towel I've been wearing on my head since it was placed there, then ball it up with my soaked things, placing them in the big ceramic basin on the antique washstand. I'll throw them in the wash tomorrow.

Even though my light fades, the familiar beam sweeps across the room, across my face, across my reflection in the mirror.

I hardly recognize myself. Again.

The tingling hits my chest through the charm, and my stomach's doing flip-flops.

I need fresh air.

In two steps I'm across the creaking, whitewashed floor, and I'm shimmying the old window up. Swoop.

Gulp. *Steady breaths, Libby. Steady breaths.*

It's gonna be okay. Frank's gonna be okay. It's not like Veronica. For one, he's sober.

For two, you weren't responsible for his life, so he's in stable hands.

Now I wanna puke.

My eyes swim with tears. The rain begins pouring in sheets again. It breaks the turning light into a hundred crystals.

Breathe. Breathe.

The light will guide them. Even if they can't see the lights of town. Even if they're navigation is sketchy. I know Frank doesn't have much on his old boat.

I take a clearing breath, focusing on the peace I felt when we arrived at the beach tonight.

The light will guide them home. I wrap my arms around myself, closing my eyes, giving my body a squeeze.

I relax. I open my eyes, welcoming the beacon like an old friend.

It turns to greet me.

Then, in a spark and a puff, it goes out.

Black.

I'm out the window, climbing down the thin metal fire escape. I practically dive off the bottom landing.

Now my feet hit the cement with a smack—stupid flip-flops—but I ignore the pangs.

Look, I have no idea if this torch is even relevant to them. But Frank's boat has nothing on it. I don't know if the Coast Guard can find him.

And right now, it's everything to me.

I'm thudding across the beach, the sand like muddy sinkholes to my feet, the rain beating me back. I can barely see my destination.

I'm at the small metal door. It's locked, but I know where my aunt keeps the spare key. Lifting it from behind a fake rock, I jam it into the lock and push inside. It's musty. The rain clatters against the outside, like beating on a drum. I reach for my flashlight and bang it against the wall, hoping to jar it. Nothing. The lighthouse is supposed to work on a generator in emergencies. *Why isn't it kicking in?* I know why. Same reason it's out.

I remember Frank told me that when they electrified the lighthouse lamp, they kept it as authentic as possible, so you could still pour in oil and light it, theoretically. I'm wearing my hoodie, the one that had Veronica's old Zippo lighter in the pocket, but I'm clueless as to how to relight the lamp without blowing myself and the lighthouse up. My need to face this ghost that knows my darkest secret, my need to do something for someone in danger for once in my life, carries me in, mimicking courage. I lift the Zippo out, flip the lid off, and spin the wheel with my thumb. Spark. Burn. I can only keep this lit for so long. It has a bit of fluid left, and a lighter like this will burn through it quickly.

I hold it up like a tiny torch. *Oil, oil . . .*

Nothing. The folded table, the display shelves with brochures, the storage door . . . *Oh.* I open it to reveal the generator being a whole bunch of worthless right now. *Where can you get spirit-proof emergency equipment?* Cleaning supplies. A bottle of oil.

It's empty.

I slam the door and begin tearing the drawers out of the cabinet. Paperwork. So much paperwork. I tug hard at a drawer, and it pops out. A phone book? Why does Sharon keep this stuff? And wires. Huh? I raise the Zippo to the rectangular gap where the drawer was, and there's a gaping hole in the wall. It's uneven, like it's been eaten through by rodents.

So maybe that's why the light's out.

Nah, it's Elizabeth.

I flip the lighter lid closed and grip the sides of the dresser to yank it away from the wall. I shake it inch by inch until I can feel around for enough space to scoot behind it. I open the Zippo again to light it. The wires look like they've been gnawed on, but not through.

The smell of lighter fluid burns my nostrils.

The flame is reflected in tiny glints and glimmers. Glass? Bottles.

I reach in, terrified that a rat is going to come flying in and chew my finger off. But rats don't fly. Right? I lift a small green container. "Nerve Tonic." I lean closer. There must be dozens of bottles filling the wall. I pull out another one: "Steady Nerves." It shows the faded image of a pretty lady on the front, a bottle in her ink-drawn hand. Beneath the picture are the words "Laudanum to Soothe All."

Laudanum. I've read enough Sherlock Holmes to know what that is. It is opium. I turn the bottle over in my hand, to the yellowed label pasted on the back.

"Prescribed to Miss Elizabeth Turnlow, one teaspoonful each hour until symptoms subside."

I gasp. Then everything goes dark as my tiny lantern burns out.

CHAPTER TWENTY-TWO

*C*rap. My eyes take a moment to adjust. In those seconds, a fuller understanding sinks into me. Elizabeth's sickness. Was she ever really sick, like physically sick?

Or was she always just sick like my sister?

My sister who wouldn't show up for a lunch date with my mom, who wouldn't call me when she said she would, who wouldn't make it to work on time some days. My sister who forgot my big birthday surprise. My sister who wouldn't wake up again because no one was there to keep her alive.

If Veronica had been in charge of a lighthouse, it would have meant disaster. Elizabeth's father knew. That's why he didn't want her to marry. He knew she needed to get well. But what does a girl in 1900 do when she's addicted to drugs? And when he got sick with pneumonia, and she was expected to take over the care of the lighthouse, who would know to stop her? I don't think my parents spoke much outside the family about my sister's addiction. How big of a secret would that have been over a hundred years ago?

"I've got it all under control." I can hear Veronica's musical voice like it's right beside me. I look. The darkness is pressing, but there's the faintest shade of light coming through the windows at the top of the tower.

I can't see a soul. My sister still won't show up for me. Why should she? I didn't show up for her, not when she needed me the most.

And Elizabeth? I'm guessing she never showed up for her captain. She wasn't there to light the torch. Not because she was punishing her big sister, sipping a freaking malt like a selfish wretch. Because she was probably drugged up and passed out.

I hear whispering. Time to go upstairs. I feel around for the metal box on the floor and grab hold. I might need it. My heart slides up and down in my chest. My body moves without my brain. It's winding and clanging upward.

Reaching the top, I look around. I can feel Elizabeth here. The whispering mixes with the sea outside.

Then I hear a door at the bottom swing open. I stare through the open trap door, down the twisting metal stairs, to the bottom.

"Libby?" Marnie. "Libby!" Sharon. They look up. "Libby," Sharon repeats. "Frank is safe."

A sob of relief pours out of me. It's startling. I'm

speechless, though, lost in the lighthouse. I came here for something.

"He's home. He fell asleep on the boat. Can you believe it? I'm making him go to bed at seven every night from here to forever . . . Libby?"

I remain silent, looking now at the dim halo spilling across the wooden floor.

She's still here.

I reach over in one movement, swinging the metal arm on the trapdoor, locking it.

This is just for me and her, the ones who killed the ones we loved.

Ice freezes across my face, my breath caught in it as her face is an inch in front of mine—no, closer.

Nose to nose with the ghost of Sayers Lighthouse.

"Libby?" The voices of my friend and aunt ring through the floor, growing more anxious.

"I'm fine," I call out to calm them.

Silence. I am definitely not fine. But once more, I can make sure others stay calm and leave me the hell alone.

"Libby, are you alone?" Sharon asks.

I bite my lip, the chill sweeping off the Lady Elizabeth, who still has not budged unless you count the slight wobbling of ectoplasm.

The ghost glances toward the box of letters I'm holding.

Elizabeth's backed away enough so I don't feel like I'm in a freezer, just a powerful refrigerator.

"You were married. You and the captain were family." The word family weighs heavy on my tongue.

The wind is rushing, screaming around the wavy glass.

"I know." The ghost doesn't move her lips, but her words fill my ears, soft and low, like an unsettling lullaby.

"So do I." I'm shaking. Am I dying? I can't seem to stop it. "And Elizabeth. Elizabeth." My face is paved with tears. I stretch my hands toward her as they shake electrically. "I forgive you." I lay the box on the ground.

"You couldn't sustain it." I take Elizabeth's hands in my own. They don't feel solid, exactly, but like something cold and charged in my grasp. I am stunned by myself. I am holding hands with a ghost. A ghost that has been haunting me since I got to Sayers. I shouldn't be here. I should be screaming. I should be running. Instead, I'm experiencing what must be some kind of freezer burn.

I dare to speak, my breath making tiny clouds. "You had no lights of your own. How could you point anyone else home?"

It almost feels like touching a cloud, or the way I thought touching a cloud might feel when I was small.

When I was more sure about my guesses.

I guessed a lot. And as the years slid by, I kept guessing wrong. About my sister. About myself.

Her light spreads, like it's spilled from a glass. It shifts from cold white to lightning-bug yellow. Like an Edison lightbulb.

I feel my necklace lift from my chest as if it's being held, admired. I can't see her face, just form, figure, reaches of light.

"I forgive you!" I sob into the light. I squeeze my eyes tight. This is it. This is where it ends.

I can smell the teakwood from the ship. Candle wax. Liquor. Lavender in a linen drawer.

I open them. She's before me, just like her picture. She's luminescent, like electric skin, touching my fingertips.

"Do you forgive me?" I cleave the words from my chest. I tear them out through my throat. We cling to each other, shadows and light, darkness and glow.

The ghost whispers back, echoing my words. "I forgive you. I forgive you."

I am rocking on my heels. I am seeing stars—actual stars. Constellations, maps, stories we tell ourselves. The bear and her sister. The vain queen.

The guiding light.

I blink, the tears straightening themselves out. The rain has stopped, but the beach outside is still black. Except for a tiny light. A green glow. I squint my eyes, my mouth open. It's a sight I know. It's moving across the shore, like it's coming from the horizon. I press my burning forehead against the cold window glass. Tiny jagged edges. Part of a star. The green is fluorescent. No, it's luminescent. Then it, too, blinks away.

Why do I smell fruity perfume and cigarettes?

"I guessed wrong about you, Elizabeth," I say the words as I turn and reach out to her. I'm startled by the hot—no, very,

very cold—tears on her face that soak my fingertips. My blue jeans. My shirt.

They're hers, and they're mine. One of us alive, one of us a wish strong enough to be real. "I guessed wrong about me, too."

"I forgive you," I repeat. She's a shattered girl. She's a blushing bride. She's a dreamer. She's a drunk.

She's my sister.

She's like an unproperly developed photo, the glow, the fuzzy detail.

The ghost's hair was dark, and now it's golden white. Her lips were set in a pale bow, now they're dark, dramatic, overdrawn.

It's me and Elizabeth. Then it's me and Veronica.

But always, it's me.

It's my chance, I think, as she shimmers back and forth between the lady of legend and my legendary sibling. *I can finally tell her.*

I open my mouth to say the words I've been desperate to say, the words that have been my only hope of forgiveness.

She faces me.

This time, my nerves are steady. This time, I can speak clearly. This time, I can almost make it right.

"I love you."

My apology has gone missing, cut off from the edge of this Polaroid. It is me and my dead sister, and . . . nothing to say sorry for.

Nothing that sorry would change, nothing that blame would mend.

"I couldn't save you alive, and you cannot save me, alive or dead." The tears blur. I wait for her reply, but all I get is silence.

It doesn't matter.

"I love you," I repeat. The picture, the face drifts into Elizabeth. "I forgive you." She smiles gently. "But you aren't here for my forgiveness, are you?"

She shakes her head slowly.

Then she changes. I see my sister again, smiling at me in a way she hadn't since we were kids at Christmas. "And you aren't here for that either, are you, Ver? You're here for me. You're here for me to forgive myself."

The ghost fades between shadows and light, a quiet glow inside the tower.

My face burns, even though my hands freeze. I can't stop crying. It feels like the tears have always been and always will be. My lips sputter with salt and snot; my head pounds. It's impossible to breathe. I have to get air.

I crank open the door from the lantern room to the platform outside. The rain is gone, but the wind pushes me back. Not as much as the dark, though. I grab hold of the railing. Something moves out of the corner of my eye.

I'm not alone out here, either.

"Lizzy." I stumble back. "Elizabeth." I laugh. "Yeah, because going outside is how you get away from ghosts. It's not as if you are a spirit who can move through walls and fly into my bedroom, or whatever, or possess a fortune-teller carnival game—that was you, right?"

Elizabeth just floats. Her eyes don't leave me.

I laugh like a decidedly crazy person. I can't get enough air. I suck in huge gulps. The chill in the wind, or the icy cling of dead girls, is burning my face and filling my eyes with tears.

I search the sky.

All the stars I saw hours before are blotted out. I can't even find Polaris now. I look back and she is gone.

I turn to see more shadows filling the lantern room. Faces from photographs. And one from my real life.

Watching the lamp.

I'm frozen in place out here on the deck, leaning against the glass. I reach as if I could touch them through the large windows.

The wind charges around me, but I swear all I hear is the wheels spinning, the gears turning in time, even as the giant lamp remains dark.

What if someone stops watching when the brightness fades? What if they don't know it will come around again?

We all stopped looking when the light left. We didn't watch for it to return.

"We went as far as our lights could take us."

Lamplight fills the room. It bursts from Elizabeth. From her captain. From my sister.

From me.

It's like a star has exploded.

The brightness shocks my eyes, and I have to shut them a moment. I shake my head and look to see the torch projecting off each shining mirror, beaming through the Fresnel lens, burning like the sun.

This is what it's like when all the lumens are working.

CHAPTER TWENTY-THREE

After I call my parents to tell them I plan to stay with Frank and Sharon for a while, they arrive with copious amounts of luggage later that week. They've rented out their own room for the rest of the summer.

"While we look for something more permanent here in Sayers," my mom says as she produces glue from her purse. "May I see your necklace?'

"What for?" I feel my half star. It doesn't tingle now—at least not in a creepy way.

Nothing about the lighthouse feels the same, even when I see a shape from time to time. Elizabeth is just looking after the lighthouse, in the way she couldn't before.

I haven't seen my sister again. I don't need to. The parts that mattered are always with me.

"It's missing a piece."

"Mom, remember? I broke it. It's always been missing half. The other side is long go—"

I stop midsentence as my mom holds Veronica's charm, the other side of the nine points, the letters *RIS* on the broken part of the banner beneath.

"You know, before you called us, we got a call from Sharon."

"I told her to let me handle it."

"But she's your aunt," my dad says, circling a small picture of a cottage for sale in the *Sayers Gazette*.

"She's nosy." I pause. "She's great." I smile. It's easy to be annoyed with Aunt Sharon. It's difficult to not love her.

"We had been waiting for someone to tell us to come up and get you. You weren't doing it." My dad folds the paper and gives me his full attention.

"Uh, I wouldn't."

"No, you wouldn't."

"Your charm? Can I see it?" My mother holds out her hand, waiting. I unfasten the clasp and pass it to her.

"Where did you find that?" I ask my mom.

"You'll never believe it. On the bed in your sister's room." I know how much it hurts her to say things like that, as if she could be talking about a living, breathing girl.

"We had to do something. We couldn't keep waiting for you to forgive us." My dad's voice shakes a little.

"What?"

"For losing Veronica. Libby, we couldn't save her. We have gone over the things we could have done, should have done . . ." My dad's eyes fill with tears. "And then, we didn't protect you."

"Dad, I have to tell you something."

I had confessed my secret to Marnie. I told Sharon. Even Nick. I spilled my guts around my aunt's kitchen table the night I confronted my ghosts, while I sipped from an oversized mug that read "Love You a Latte."

I take a breath. "I lied for her. I didn't want her to leave and go to rehab. I thought she would get better. I thought we could finally be close. Veronica counted on me. She depended on me to make sure she was up every afternoon. And I told her I could handle it."

My dad's face is blank, and then understanding spreads over it. My mother nods and takes his hand.

"We know, baby."

"How?"

"We suspected, when you had an alarm go off at the same time every day, always with some excuse. And I snooped in your phone. After. We should have caught it before. Protected you."

"Protected me?"

"We knew Ver was gone, but we were afraid we'd lose you, too. You were so eager to be close to her. We didn't know how to draw the line. We didn't know what to say or do."

"You've been worried about protecting *me*?"

"That's why we sent you here. To help you get away from everything. To heal. We knew it was too difficult to be around us."

"I thought you couldn't take the sight of me." I say it so softly I'm surprised they hear me. But they do. I'm strangled in a hug. They won't let go. I don't mind it.

"There's a two-bedroom down the street from me," Marnie tells me on our way back from a meeting. Nick's flipping through my pictures; I'm flipping through his. Photos of shorebirds and lobstermen. An awkward Polaroid of me and my family. It's the midsummer-night lobster boil, and my necklace is obnoxiously green.

Now I wear the whole charm. Glowing, but clearly damaged. Whole and bright and scarred. A waxy line of glue runs up along the seam where the star fuses together.

I'm taking my light as far as it can go.

ACKNOWLEDGMENTS

Thank you to my wonderful husband for his endless support and patience. Thank you to my daughter for telling strangers about my books and pushing people to buy them.

Huge thanks to Kate Gregor, Renae Smith, DeAnn Karnes, Anabella Walker, and Jennifer Walker for offering instrumental feedback.

Thank you so much to Kerry Winkelmann.

I am always grateful to the fabulous Nicole Ayers of Ayers Edits. You are making me a better writer.

Thank you to my parents, always. You shared Maine with me.

Thank you to the Katahdin Inn.

I love the designs of Kimberley Marsot with KimG Designs, and this cover might be my favorite. Thank you.

Thank you to Katherine Trail of KT Editing Services for making my book's guts pretty.

And thank you to my readers.
Thank you forever.

PLAYLIST

Them Shoes by Patrick Sweany

Some of Adam's Blues by The Quaker City Night Hawks

Brandy by Looking Glass

Narrow Mind by Claude Hay

Tomorrow, Wendy by Concrete Blonde

Hurricane by Band of Heathens

Wreck of the Edmund Fitzgerald by Gordon Lightfoot

House on a Hill by Passenger

ABOUT THE AUTHOR

Mary Jane Capps writes young adult novels about witches, mermaids, and ghosts – or some combination of the three.

She likes to keep things spooky, magical, and reasonably upbeat.

Mary Jane lives in Fort Mill, South Carolina with her husband and daughter, down the road from her parents, in a house that is probably haunted.

Sign up for book info and fun giveaways
at www.maryjanecapps.com

facebook.com/storytellingspark

instagram.com/maryjanecapps